Knockabeg
A Famine Tale

Knockabeg
A Famine Tale

by Mary E. Lyons

Houghton Mifflin Company
Boston 2001

www.houghtonmifflinbooks.com

The text of this book is set in Horley Old Style.

Library of Congress Cataloging-in-Publication Data
Lyons, Mary E.
Knockabeg: a famine tale / by Mary E. Lyons.
p. cm.
Summary: The faeries of Knockabeg become involved in the Irish potato famine
as they wage war on each other.
ISBN 0-618-09283-8
[1. Fairies—Fiction. 2. Ireland—History—Famine, 1845–1852—Fiction.
3. Famines—Ireland—Fiction.] I. Title.
PZ7.L99556 Kn 2001
[Fic]—dc21
00-066974
Manufactured in the United States of America
QUM 10 9 8 7 6 5 4 3 2 1

This story is dedicated to the memory of
James Lyons, 1874–1950,
my great-uncle and the first of us
born in America.

Acknowledgments
I am grateful to Art Collier and Jane Smith for
their sensitive insights about the faery world; my
husband, Paul Collinge, a master of faery logic;
and Emma and Haley, my faery assistants.

Contents

I am the *seanchaí*. The storyteller. Holder of history, keeper of tales. I'm ancient, 'tis true, but remember — the older the fiddle, the sweeter the tune.

So. Hand me my pipe, and gather your toes 'round the hearth. It's this I'm wanting to tell ye: a story of hunger and magic in the land of West Isle.

Hallow Eve, Dusk

This is the way it was.

They planned to meet, as usual, on Hallow Eve. Deep inside the mountains of Knockabeg, weeshy men and women fastened their capes, then pulled on belled red caps. 'Tis these caps that make the creatures invisible, you understand.

After the going under of the sun, when dusk glazed the air, the clan headed to the tower by the sea. Someone with an ear to the ground might have heard paw-sized brogues skip down secret paths. Three feet at a time, they hopped over stiles and bridges to reach the cliff where the tower stood.

So many faeries! And in such a hurry, they almost hurtled over the edge into waves that gnashed far below. But faeries don't fall unless they want to. Truth to tell, faeries do only what pleases them. Or what the Queen commands.

The Wee Ones took a moment's rest, plucked owl feathers from their caps, and spread them on the wet grass. Oh, 'twas good to be together again! After all, these were the Trooping Faeries — a close-knit group that liked to visit and gossip.

For this reason, they often did their mischief in bands of twosies or threesies, most especially on Hallow Eve. *Ach*, Hallow Eve! On this night, the last before winter's chill, the faeries would dance in the tower to a faery harp.

What a sight! Wee folk whirling so wildly that many would land on the rafters and hang there, light as cobwebs. At dawn they would toast the Queen, every acorn cup filled with dewdrops. 'Twas a delicious nectar that always brought a mortal to his knees.

If a mortal were invited. One faery, a particularly pudgy fellow sitting at the back of the field, started a rumor. "I hear Herself has gone daft over the mortals' potato crop. That's why no flesh and blood will be at the ball this night."

"So, who cares about mortals?" one of his neighbors answered. "Who cares? This is our ball, anyway."

"Shush!" said another. "The Queen has arrived."

As buttons of starlight appeared, the Queen jumped through the crowd. Soon she was standing in front of them, next to a mound of stones ten feet high. The cairn was a giant's grave, some said, yet no one knew for sure.

It had been there since before faery memory began. Before they thought themselves higher than God, and He pushed them from Above-the-Sky. Knocked senseless from the fall, the Trooping Ones awoke to find themselves on West Isle, stuck on Earth and halfway to Under-the-Ground.

Because the Queen had a grim message to deliver, she decided to speak from the top of the cairn. Tonight of all nights, she wanted to look as queenish as possible. And the truth was, the Queen had always been a bit sensitive about her height, not to mention her poor eyesight.

Well, she sighed to herself. *I am* taller than most . . . a *good two feet if I stretch my neck.* "Steps!" she commanded. "Step to!"

Three members of High Council quickly appeared, looking quite important. Each wore a scarlet cloak with his initial embroidered on the lapel. The Step called Jam threw his roly-poly body on the ground in front of the cairn. The others, Mungo and Wink, lay down on top of Jam, forming a staircase for the Queen.

As she ascended, Mungo groaned. "Begob, the old girl gets heavier every year." Mungo was a whiner, but he was wise, so the Queen put up with him.

"Mind your tongue," said Wink. "It's a privilege to be stepped on by the Queen." Wink had no imagination, but he was steady as rain, so she put up with him, too.

"You would think that, since you're on top," Mungo replied.

Jam, being on the bottom, could say nothing at all. Every time High Council met, he agreed with everything the Queen said. And because all queens need a Jam to make them feel clever, he had been there from the beginning.

While a piper played "The Faery Queen," the Queen scrambled up the rocks. Immediately the Steps unfolded themselves and stood at attention. The faeries stopped their chattering, spellbound by the spangles that twinkled from their leader's cloak. When she reached the top of the cairn, she put on her glasses and faced the crowd. "God save all here!"

"God save our Queen! God save our Queen!" the Wee

Ones answered. Their voices silvered the darkening air, though Knockabeg mortals heard only ruffles of wind from the sea.

A voice from the back squealed. "If God had wanted to save us, we wouldn't be here."

The Queen scowled. She couldn't see the speaker, but she knew the voice. Sticky! All faeries are full of tricks and insults, but Sticky was worse than most because she was smarter than most. Though she sat on High Council, she had been a member for only five winters, so the Queen usually ignored her disrespect.

"Good People," the Queen called out. "You will not be having a ball tonight. Indeed, all holidays have been cancelled until further notice."

A shray! shray! shray! of protest rose from the troupe. The faeries' faces, full of delight a moment before, now looked like old gray turnips.

Sticky shrieked with laughter. "Let the Queen wiggle out of this one!"

The Queen raised both arms. "There is more." The shrays turned to softer slih, slih, slihs.

"You must have noticed the fields around Knockabeg this past month. You have seen the blackened potato stalks and the tubers rotting in the ground."

"Smelled them, smelled them!" one faery screeched.

Sticky held her nose. "Pee-yew!"

To their credit, Jam, Wink, and Mungo kept straight faces, but all the other Wee Ones jiggled with laughter. The

Queen was exasperated. Would they never grow up, these faeries of hers? The path back to Above-the-Sky was unclear, even to her. Yet surely they could not take the first step until they stopped their selfish ways.

Now the Queen was shouting. "Mortals sell most of their cabbage and turnips at market. The hard-working cotter eats eight pounds of potatoes a day. His wife eats four, the children two. Praties are all they have."

"Yah, yah, yah," chanted the flock. "Cotters bring home shillings from the market. Shillings from the market!"

"Whisht, you fools! The shillings go to Lord Armitage Shank for his bloody rent! Many families have even sold their hide canoes and fishing nets to pay the fee. If there are no potatoes to harvest, our mortals will starve this winter."

The Queen removed her glasses and squinted hard at the crowd.

"Look under the coats they wear to market. You will see only rags. And under the rags, no more flesh than that of a wren. Old Molly who lives alone on Mully Mountain is already yellow from hunger. She has so little food that her stomach is eating itself."

"What's it to us? What's it to us?" the faeries yelled.

The Queen thought quickly. "Without potatoes, a family must eat its hen. That means no eggs by the door at dawn for you. When the chicken is gone, they kill the cow. No piggin of buttermilk on the windowsill at dusk. And when the oat sack is empty, you will find not a scrap of oaten bread in any human pocket to keep your belly full."

The wind died down as the Wee People considered this fearful threat. Even Sticky grew quiet for a moment, but, being a disagreeable sort, she decided to disagree.

Sticky was an unremarkable-looking faery—short-haired, bowlegged, and only one foot tall. A creature of odd habits, she always wore gloves of dried sea foam. Even stranger, she avoided large groups of faeries at the re-unions—aye, was often seen pulling her cap over her ears in a most unsociable way.

Still, Sticky had an unusually deep voice, and she knew how to use it. Yanking off her cap, she moved to the front of the assembly and climbed halfway up the cairn. "Stop worrying! Potato crops often fail in Knockabeg. Black Leg, Leaf Curl—the people are used to potato disease. Remember the Dear Summer, when praties rotted in the pit? The Spring of Storms, when the tubers never grew? No matter how hungry humans get, they always leave a crumb or two for us."

The Wee Ones patted their potbellies. "Aye, aye. A crumb or two for us."

The Queen was hoarse now, and desperate. "This famine will be much worse than those others! It appears to be . . . it seems . . . I feel sure it is a curse."

*O-o-o-h-h-oh*s of pain escaped from the clan, as if each had been pierced by a grass-blade sword.

"Return to your mountain homes," the Queen directed. "Put your castles and caves in order. Then pack a squirrel-skin pouch with faery darts. We will meet here again at dusk tomorrow. Bring a stout cabbage stump, and, above all, do not forget the darts."

The faeries, utterly silent, seemed unable to move. Whatever did their leader have in mind? The Queen swallowed tears she hoped no one could see. Aroo, it was hard to be in charge! She lowered her voice and gave them the chilling news.

"Good People, the Nuckelavees have been here. We are going to war."

Hallow Eve, Midnight

The sound of a faery mob is a harsh one, indeed. The Queen's words set off a frenzy of bells as the Wee Ones shook their heads. They cried and squealed and stomped their waushy leather shoes until the mortals of Knockabeg awoke to rumbles of thunder.

Jam looked up at the Queen. "Steps?" he shouted.

She shook her head. The tinkling bells of her own cap were drowned by the riot below. "No time!"

The Queen motioned for Jam to help her descend. She then went out among the rabble, remembering to lift her chin and extend her neck. With the dignity of a swan she glided through the field. The Steps, meanwhile, kept a close watch on the crowd.

For hours, the Queen softly murmured faery phrases that meant "have courage" and "be of strong heart." And by midnight, the Wee Ones were calm. Exchanging faint goodbyes of "clah clah," they stuck the owl feathers back in their caps and peacefully trooped home.

Quite overcome, the Queen returned to the cairn and leaned against it. "High Council, assemble now behind the tower. I need a moment's rest. In ten leaps of a salmon, I will join you."

Wink collapsed with relief, his legs as limp as seaweed.

He knew his job was to defend the Queen, but he never imagined he might have to fight one of his own kind.

The plump Jam helped Wink to his feet. "Up you go, up you go. We've more work to do."

Mungo looked around for Sticky. "Bedad! Where is she? The woman has not a splink of sense." Then he saw her, teetering on the edge of the cairn.

"Sticky, you've been up there all this time? Why, you're paler than a *pooka*!"

"Nuckelavees," the faery woman mumbled. "What does the Queen know of Nuckelavees?"

Sticky grabbed Mungo's hand and picked her way down the stones. Together they hopped to the rear of the tower, where Wink and Jam were waiting at the very edge of the cliff, three hundred feet above the sea. They were a nervous group, they were. Jam tilted his neck and scanned the dark skies above. Stroking the *S* on her cape, Sticky stared out at the water, as if seeking the answer to a question.

Wink twisted the buttons on his checked vest. "Never been to battle before, never been to battle. Never shot a dart at naught but cattle. Only cattle." His chin quivered while he tried to picture himself in combat.

"Hwee! Hwee!" said Mungo, laughing. "Wink, you should try to be more like Father Gallagher." Mungo thought this a clever cut. Father Gallagher was the Knockabeg priest — a confident man who was overly impressed with himself.

But only Sticky laughed at Mungo's joke. Most Wee

Ones were afraid of Gallagher. They knew the priest preached against them in Sunday sermons. If he had his way, he would cork them in a bottle and rid Knockabeg of faeries for good.

"Leave Wink be," said Jam. He looked at the sky again. Storm clouds of *pookas* had already gathered, waiting for the ball to begin. Hallow Eve was the only festival when ghosts danced with faeries. Who would tell them the ball was cancelled? Jam knew he didn't have the nerve — *pookas* were too easily annoyed.

Jam turned to Wink. "Don't fret. If we obey the Queen, we'll be safe." And Jam believed this with all his heart.

The Queen flew around the corner of the tower, quick as a swallow. As she landed, she dabbed a pearl of sweat from her upper lip — the only sign that she had just survived the greatest crisis of her reign. The leader settled upon a white quartz rock reserved especially for royal rumps. The others moved in close to form a circle, one bony knee touching the other.

"Since harvest began, I have examined this potato blight," the Queen began. "Why some fields and not others? I asked myself. Why some vines, but not all?"

"Maybe you forgot your glasses," Sticky said.

"Shut up," spat Jam.

"I rode around the entire coast of West Isle last night," continued the Queen. "Long hours I spent on my cabbage-stump horse, searching for some creature bent on destruction — a giant, perhaps, or a *pooka* gone off his head. But I was looking with the wrong eyes. Once I narrowed my gaze, the Nuckelavees were easy to find by the light of the moon.

"Tens of thousands I saw, though they flew in singles. Each no more than six inches tall, but beautiful beyond words. They cruised a foot above the ground, exhaling spittles of fog. When they sped away, I heard low calls of 'tattheration, tattheration.' 'Twas a gurgly sound, as if clumps of oatmeal were stuck in their throats."

The Destruction Curse, thought Sticky with dread.

"By dawn," the Queen went on, "every potato vine in their paths was covered by fog. When the white stuff rolled away, many of the fields were a stinking, oozing mess. Saddest of all were the mortal families."

The Queen's voice buckled with grief. "As I neared home, I saw *mamais* crouched in the middle of fields. Some had babes in their arms. The daddies, stooped as old men, paced squares of sorrow around the stone-wall boundaries. They had been there all night, trying to guard their land against more blight."

Sticky hooted. "*Their* land? Don't you mean Lord Shank's land that his ancestors stole from the people?" Oh, she did love to catch the Queen in a mistake!

"Whatsomever. Our problem is this. All I know about Nuckelavees is what the former King told me, God rest his soul. That they are part of the winged faery species known as Solitary Ones.

"Like other Solitary Ones—Willy Wisps, Mermen, Sheerie, Gray Men—they were banished from Above-the-Sky and landed on East Isle. But of all the Solitary Ones,

11

Nuckelavees spin the worst magic. Indeed, they are barbarous invaders. Why they choose to attack West Isle mortals now is a puzzle."

Sticky thought she knew—yes, yes, she did. East Isle must be ruined, she felt certain of it.

The Queen's gaze rested on her. "Any ideas, Sticky?"

"I'm sure we cannot win this war!"

Wink moaned. "I can't imagine how we'll fight the Nuckelavees if they attack in singles. Their numbers are too many."

"You are right to declare war, Your Honor," said Jam. "But if the Nuckelavees are as small as you say, we're done for. The moon won't always be on our side. Like the midges that chew on mortal necks, these faeries will be impossible to see."

"Mungo, what thoughts have you?" asked the Queen.

As wise faeries usually do, Mungo deliberated before he answered. "Is there a choice? We won't survive if our mortals die. If we move to Frog Leg Island, perhaps we can stop the Nuckelavees before they reach West Isle again."

The Queen nodded. "Should I take the Weapon of Last Resort?"

Jam's double chin dropped. "Not the horn, Your Honor! That would be most unsafe."

"Aye," the Queen replied unhappily. "But if it comes to that . . ."

"I suppose we must kidnap a human," said Wink with pride, for he seldom had an idea of his own. "We'll need a strong mortal arm to fight with us and to steal our food."

The Queen turned to Sticky. "You are Faery Guardian to a family who lives next to the bridge. Their ten-year-old lad is a shepherd, amn't I right?"

Sticky's mouth went dry as rust. Not Eamon! Why not some useless boy like Frankie Blaine—a cruel, pock-marked lad who pulled wings off of dragonflies just for the fun in it.

"I've watched Eamon climb up the cliffs to fish," said the Queen. "Heard his laughter when he chases sheep to the fold. He is a brave, lighthearted fellow, is he not?"

"Yes, but perhaps you wouldn't want him now. His da drowned last spring. The boy has been a wandering lost soul since then."

"Well and good. That makes our magic even easier. I've a stash of enchanted herring in my reticule. Tonight, roast the fish and leave them by his shepherd's crook. When he finds them at dawn, he'll have a feast. As thin as he is, I've no doubt of his appetite."

Sticky nodded.

"Then quickly, after he is under the spell but before the sun fully rises, bring him to my castle to sleep it off. Tomorrow night he travels with us." The Queen frowned. Why was Sticky so quiet?

"No arguments?"

"None, Your Honor."

"Mungo, you go with her. See that she succeeds, for you know the rules. *Deenee Shee* cannot fight without a mortal by our side. Or eat food unless a mortal gives it to us first."

"Yes, ma'am." Mungo tried not to show his doubt. It

wasn't that he didn't like Sticky. Her peculiar appearance had touched him since the first day she wandered into Mully Mountain. In pitiful need of a new dress and hairstyle, she'd had nothing to her name save a rose thorn needle and a silver comb.

Sticky said she'd been living alone in a cave far up the glen. That she was glad to finally find her clan. This much was true, for from the start, Sticky had helped both faeries and mortals. Her needle mended many a Trooping slipper, and when Willy Wisps infested Knockabeg, only Sticky knew what to do.

One night she climbed the tower and called magic words toward the sea. After the Wisps were gone, ocean lights that tricked mortals into walking off the cliff melted, too. Yet Sticky was often rude to the Queen, so Mungo was surprised when she made Sticky the High Council member-at-large. And sometimes the newcomer seemed ill at ease with Trooping magic. This worried him now.

What about the night they sneaked into a wedding party to steal a mortal bride? Mungo had tossed invisible pepper at the bride and waited. Three sneezes from her without a "God bless," and the comely girl would have been his to keep forever.

Then what did Sticky do but knock over a noggin of whiskey, which spilled on the cottage floor, which soaked the foot of an old woman, who said "God bless!" just as the bride sneezed a third time. So now he, handsome Mungo, still lived alone in his fine castle under a blackthorn bush.

Well, he would find out soon enough if his friend could

handle the assignment. Soon and after a while, he and Sticky would kidnap the mortal boy. For now, there was still much to do. Mungo must carve a set of arrow-shaped darts, and Sticky had to dig a roasting pit for the herring.

Following usual custom, the High Council escorted the Queen home. Except for a few owl feathers, which puffed over the ground like scraps of sheep's wool, the faery fields were empty. The *pookas* had already left to haunt another tower, as it's a well-known fact that no ghost worth his death sheet will waste a perfectly good Hallow Eve.

For one dazzling moment, the moon tossed sapphires of light across the sea. Then that glow dimmed, and the tower stood alone and friendless in the dark.

"Ah, would you just look at him?" Sticky cooed.

"Glsipw," replied Mungo, whose mouth was full. The two faeries were sitting on the hearth in Eamon's kitchen. They shared a three-legged wooden creepy, a very small little mite of a wee stool. Its seat was oddly shaped — four sides, none the same length — but it was just right for a pair of elfish backsides. 'Twas the only furnishing in the one-room place, save for an oaken table and kitchen dresser.

"Look at him. Curled up with his wee sister in front of the fire." Since the pair had entered the cottage, Sticky's eyes had not left Eamon's sleeping face for a moment.

Mungo hated gushiness. "Yes, and there's Granny in the outshot, snoring like a pig." He oinked. "And Mamaí in the cow byre, gurgling like . . ."

"Blast you, Mungo! This is *my* mortal family. Find your own humans to make fun of." The faery woman gave a shove with her hip and tried to push him off the stool.

Mungo stopped chewing the bread that Granny left for the faeries every night. He took a long look at Sticky's face. After five winters, he was slowly getting used to her moods — her sarcasm, her need to be alone. Even her grumpiness at faery reunions. At the last May Eve celebration, she'd plugged her ears with sea beans and wouldn't talk to anyone!

But now Mungo saw some new thing in her face. Determination, was it? Or pride perhaps? Just then, Eamon's little sister mewled in her sleep.

"*Ach,* the wee urchin has the hunger on her," said Sticky. "It's she who should be eating herring."

Still asleep, Eamon spread his arm and lifted the blanket so it covered five-year-old Hannah's shoulders. *Such a thin arm,* Sticky thought, *but as strong as a shovel.*

Mungo extended a lizard-size tongue and delicately nabbed a bread crumb from his forefinger. "Why isn't she sleeping with her *mamaí*?"

"Poor woman's not right in the head since the da died. Eamon puts his hand to everything now. As well he should, for I'll need . . .

"Many's the day I've seen Eamon at the bog with the menfolk, and him still a growing lad," she quickly said. "He cuts turf all day. When it's dry, he hauls it home in a basket slung over his slender back. Plants and digs the potatoes, turnips, cabbages. Whitewashes the cottage and thatches the roof, too.

"But the boy needs to grow a good bit." Sticky's voice burned with impatience. "When it's time to weight the thatch, he has to wait for his Uncle Jimmy to row around from Kiltymore."

"Jimmy the Fiddler?"

"Aye. Jimmy throws hay ropes over the roof. Eamon ties them to iron pins at the top of the walls. You should see the knots. Fine tight ones his da taught him to make for the fishing nets."

Mungo shuddered when he heard the word *iron*. Iron and direct sunbeams were harmful to faeries. Just three dusks ago, he'd had a run-in with the mortal William Blaine. Blaine owned a shop at the crossroads, the only one in Knockabeg. After he refused to sell oats on credit to the Widow Sweeney, Mungo decided to punish the meal monger. The widow and her daughter, May, were rickles of skin and bones! What kind of mortal would deny them food?

But when Mungo's dart punctured Blaine's best cow, the storekeeper sought revenge. Before Mungo could holler "Horo," Blaine tied a horseshoe around the animal's neck to protect it from another faery blow. Mungo's head still ached from the sight of the iron shoe.

Hannah whimpered again, and Eamon stirred.

"Ah, he's waking now," said Mungo. "He'll soon be out and about. To the field with us, Sticky. Remember, we must do this quickly. The Queen expects the boy by day-clear."

"You go ahead." Sticky seemed as calm as a grazing ewe. "Take the herring out of the roasting pit. It should be well done by now. You'll find Eamon's crook resting on a boulder at the sunset side of the field. I'll wait here to make sure he follows the smell of the fish."

Mungo raised an eyebrow. His friend was altogether too serene. Sticky pushed him onto the earthen floor. "Get on with you, or the herring will be too chewy to eat."

Still a touch doubtful, Mungo hopped out of the cottage door and headed to the field. Even in the dim light of dawn, he could see that the family rented only one rood of potato ground. The quarter acre was scarcely bigger than the faery fort on top of Mully Mountain, which the Wee Ones sometimes used as a hurling field.

On the sunrise side of the field, a low wall of loose stones divided Eamon's patch from William Blaine's sizeable plot. *Poor slip of a lad,* thought Mungo. *What cruel bad luck to have Blaine as a neighbor.*

Another wall ran down the sunset side. Past this, the land sloped to a stony shore and a narrow harbor. Beyond the harbor, a great mantle of ocean spread out to the west. Only the rocky spine of an island in the far distance broke the surface of the water. Devil's Rock, the mortals called it.

Mungo could just make out the piles of black seaweed and shells of broken canoes that littered the harbor shore. "Glic, glic," he murmured. "The sun will be full up soon!"

Faster than two rolls of a stone, he leapt to the roasting pit, filled his hands with herring, and sped to the boulder where Eamon kept the crook. *Hurry, Sticky, hurry,* he thought.

If this mission failed, the Queen would be furious, and if Sticky didn't care, Mungo did. He didn't want to lose his seat on High Council. Even more, he didn't want to give up the council livery. The crimson cloak well suited his ruddy complexion, and he prized the *M* on the lapel.

But Mungo had seen the last of Sticky for a while. At the very moment he was racing around the field, she was pulling two lightly roasted herrings from her pocket. When she tossed them outside the cottage door, Eamon's nose twitched and his mouth watered. Gum-eyed from sleep, he crawled to his feet and raked the turf coals in the fire. *A dream of food, is it?* he wondered. *Or is it my empty belly that's tricked me stomach? I smell roasted fish!*

Sticky looked out the cottage window, which was barely bigger than a lord's handkerchy. Already the sky was pinking up. "Make haste!" she ordered the boy.

Eamon heard nothing, though he did feel a slight prickle in his ear. Sticky stomped on the lad's bare toes. "Thank God you've got no shoes to put on, and no clothes but the woolen rags you slept in!"

Rubbing his itching feet, Eamon took a rush candle from the cranny built into the chimney wall. He thrust the rush into the smoldering turf until the tallow caught. Candle in hand, he opened the door and peered outside.

"*Ach!*" he cried when he saw Sticky's herring a'laying on the ground like an unclaimed prize. Then, without a care for sickly Mamaí or frail Granny or tiny Hannah, Eamon picked up the fish and stuffed them in his mouth. For he had a great power of hunger, you see, which ofttimes is stronger than anything, even love.

As Eamon swallowed, all memory of the herring left his mind, and he fell to the ground in a dark slumber.

Sticky jerked a length of straw from the roof. She tucked him safely under her arm (she couldn't carry him too low, you understand, for the boy's feet would drag through the brambles, or too high, for the rising sun might toast his hair) and cried, "My horse! My bridle! My saddle!"

The straw turned into a white steed strong enough to whisk Sticky and Eamon to Devil's Rock. When Mungo looked up to check the progress of the sun, he saw the horse zigzag above him. His mouth opened so wide that a thrush could have nested there.

"Let the Queen go off to war," Sticky shouted as she passed overhead. "But she'll not take the boy with her. He's mine, I tell you — mine!"

For the rest of that day, our faery woman was in a tart mood, indeed. Deep inside a cave on Devil's Rock, she argued with herself. Her only company was the roar of waves that cupped the island and her befuddled thoughts.

Certainly she felt no loyalty to the Queen, not having been brought up to it, do you see. In truth, the Queen was just too perfect to suit Sticky. All that patience and kindness! But for Sticky to desert her friend Mungo and the High Council — now that was a rat of a different fur.

The faery comforted herself by stripping off her tight gloves — what a relief! Smiling, she watched Eamon's sleeping face and thought of the pleasant life she would soon enjoy with him by her side.

She then turned her attention to a stubborn pile of turf. As a rule, faeries don't burn peat fires, but she was anxious to keep her lad warm until the army left that night. Only then would she return him to his cabin.

A spark flickered when Sticky snapped her fingers over the turf. "Light, blast you!" She kicked a lump of the soft black peat, thinking it reminded her of hairy black boogers she'd once seen hanging in a Merman's nose.

Just as the flame died, a piggly voice bounced off the walls of the cave. "What do you expect, when you use fresh-cut turf?"

Sticky inhaled sharply and tried to see through the darkness. "Who is it? Who's there?"

The owner of the voice threw his cabbage stump on the ground outside the cave and marched into the solid blackness, hands on hips. "The lumps haven't had time to dry."

"Mungo!" Sticky scrambled to her feet. "It's after dusk. Isn't the army gathering now?"

"I'll not leave without you. Cripes, it's cold in here."

"Lower your voice, or the boy's ears will itch, and he'll wake. Now be good enough to loan me your cloak. He's in a bad state of shivering."

Mungo unhooked the pearly buttons on his cape, then tucked it like a napkin around Eamon's neck. The scent of faery seeped into the boy's dreams. It held a hint of brine, like sea air or the sweat of a small child.

"We need you, Sticky," said Mungo. "Since day fall the Queen's army has been weaving sky nets from seaweed. Jam thinks we can catch thousands of the boogies in the air and shoot them with darts."

Sticky sat down wearily by the dead fire. Mungo crouched beside her. "When we didn't produce Eamon this morning, the Queen almost ripped off my *M*. She calmed down after Jam stole William Blaine's son, Frankie. Rolled the boy out of bed and thumped him until he was fully faery-struck. But that young buck-o may be too spoiled to do us much good at all, at all."

Sticky rubbed her eyes. An aching was coming on her head. "Listen, my friend. You'll need more than twelve-year-old Frankie to win this war. Nuckelavees live only to create a wicked world where they can feel at home. Apparently they've spoilt East Isle. Now they need to conquer new territory."

Yerra! thought Mungo. *How did she know so much about these Nuckelavees?* The slumbering Eamon trembled. Again Sticky snapped her fingers over the turf. "Begonies!"

"Here," Mungo suggested, "let's try together."

Their four faery fists, each the size of a mussel, struck a dazzling spark, and the turf finally lit. But in the last second of darkness, Mungo noticed a black, gold-flecked stain on the inside of his friend's hands.

"Sticky, what in God's name?"

He opened her palms, and though he rubbed and kneaded, the shiny stain remained as if it had grown into her skin.

"Let go, Mungo! Some things are too private to share."

Just then, a horse's hooves clattered across the top of the cave. In the next moment, a small face gleeked from the entrance. "Mungo?" a dony voice called.

It was Jam. A wad of netting was strapped to his back, and lengths of seaweed trailed to the ground. Polka dots of excitement reddened his cheeks. "I thought I recognized your cabbage stump outside. We leave for Frog Leg Island immediately.

"I left formation just to find you," he added, vexed that he'd had to break the Queen's rule about staying together.

"If we go now, we can still catch up. I'll wait exactly sixty winks of a bird's eye. Not one more." Jam sniffed and waddled out of the cave.

Mungo pulled his cloak from Eamon's neck. "Come, Sticky, come," he begged. "Why do you desert us now?"

"Perhaps one day I can tell you. For now, I will say only that a rope cannot be made of sea sand. Go, and safe journey to you and Jam."

Baffled, Mungo shook his head. He gave a sharp salute, marched out of the cave, and mounted his cabbage. "My horse!" he cried. "My bridle! My saddle!"

The two warriors headed east through a keyhole in the clouds. Mungo was certain he would soon see Sticky again, and Sticky was just as certain of her own future.

She knew it soon after coming to Knockabeg, when she first saw five-year-old Eamon playing at the foot of Mully Mountain. Even at that young age, the lad's legs were long, and his arms were as hard as the firwood that mortals dug from the bog. *He's the very one!* the faery woman had thought.

So. For five years, Sticky waited. Now Eamon was ten and almost tall enough for her to carry out the plan. But the truth is, none of us, even faeries, knows what the morrow will bring. We think it is ours to command, then it turns and sticks out its tongue. And isn't that just the way of it?

November–December

Nothing could have prepared the Wee Ones for the trip to Frog Leg Island. Squally weather made the ride a rocky one, and only a few had the foresight to bring umbrellas. The rain was so heavy that soon these stalks of Queen Anne's Lace were in tatters and turned quite inside out.

Bitter were the curses when the Wee Ones finally saw their destination below. Frog Leg lay far out at sea, halfway between West and East Isles. The place was more fit for goats than faeries, for the weather was bleak and the land stony. The few mortals who lived there scratched out a meager life, indeed.

But the Queen's army soon found its mettle. As autumn marched into winter, they built bark tents in an abandoned cemetery. Supply depots were established, and yards of seaweed netting were tightly knotted.

These tasks out of the way, the Trooping Ones started basic training. At dusk they ran up High Peak, the steepest hill on the island. Most were winded by the time they reached the top, as hopping doesn't prepare a faery for jogging, you see. And that was only the start of the nightly workout.

Once they reached High Peak, Jam led the calisthenics: belly-ups, thumb-presses, and jumping micks. These last are similar in style to mortals' jumping jacks, save for a smaller range of motion.

He had a clever head, me Jam, and contrived at first to avoid most of the exercises. But the other faeries weren't long under the deception. After a few nights, they forced the chubby Step to join them. Soon he, too, was taut as a cat.

Around midnight, the Wee Ones ran back to the cemetery for dart practice. Wink was in charge, and he took right away to it, oh, he did. "It's me'll make the short work o'ye!" he liked to yell at the troops. "Now, then. Who'll trap us a nice box o'rats?"

This business with the rats was a terrible one out and out. The fearless thugs were one foot long, with sharp teeth and beady eyes. They were easy enough to find, as they stalked the island in droves, but few faeries had the stomach to meet one face to face.

Yet every night some shivering volunteer crawled through the fields with a broom and bark box. Meanwhile, the other soldiers waited atop the stone wall that encircled the graveyard. When the volunteer returned with his catch, Wink ordered him to release the beasts. "Ready!" he cried from a safe distance. "Aim! Throw!"

The Wee Ones came to despise these sessions, and let it be said that several darts misfired, whizzing dangerously close to Wink's rear end.

Mungo organized the most important drill of all: teaching Wee Ones to follow orders. Shortly before dawn, when herds of seals sliced through the sea, he took the faeries to a low spot on the strand. The Step then led his troops into the freezing waters, where each climbed on the back of a seal.

"Mount! Left! Right! Under! Over!" Mungo called. "Dismount! Remount! Remember — keep your caps on your heads!"

Frankie Blaine did not care for any of the training at all, most especially the cold water. After only one night of jogging and throwing and swimming, he approached Mungo. The young hooligan's eyes were two hard peas of hate. "I'm sick of this tomfoolery! Take me home!"

Mungo didn't want to anger the boy too much, as they needed him greatly. "Steady now. I'll release you from training on two conditions. You must work on the ruling of your tongue, and you must find food for us."

This suited the lad better, for he fancied himself a great flatterer. He loved stealing, too, and why not, he being his father's son? The next morning, Frankie stood quite haughty before the largest tent in the cemetery. He shoved his big foot inside the door. "Please to see the Queen!"

Jam reached out and twisted the boy's foot. "Who disturbs Her Honor in broad daylight?"

Frankie squealed in pain. "How dare the likes of you speak like that to the likes of me? Just wait till my father hears about this."

Sighing, for she had been organizing squadrons all night, the Queen peeked out of the tent. With a simpering smile, Frankie presented his take: one hogshead of oatmeal, three noggins of goat's milk, four baskets of eggs, five barrels of dried herring, and ten flitches of smoked bacon.

The Queen cleaned her glasses and looked again.

"Frankie Blaine, are ye cracked? Ye've stolen most of the food on the island! Faeries require but little to eat. My supply officers will bury the herring. You must return the rest."

Frankie bowed. "Yes, Your Majesty and Highness and Greatness."

"Imph, I'm fed up with you, Frankie. Take your brazen self away from me." With a flip of her cape, the Queen slammed the tent door on Frankie's sore foot.

So. Frankie returned the food, and that night he was tied to a gravestone with only two herrings to eat and rainwater to drink. The lad couldn't stir as much as a toenail, and didn't it put him in a temper? In troth, Frankie was not having much of a holiday with the faeries.

Well, God be good to him. It's a lucky thing Frankie couldn't see the future, else he'd have begged to stay on Frog Leg forever.

New Year's Eve

It must be said that Sticky sometimes wished she were with the others. The faery had set herself a hard task, oh, she had. While the Trooping Ones trained on Frog Leg, she forced herself to sit on Eamon's roof every night. She would have preferred the comfort of her own cave, of course, but the stakes were too high.

And by New Year's Eve, she was feeling uneasy in her mind. On that night, she listened with big ears to a discussion below. It proved that keeping Eamon well fed would be difficult, indeed.

"Towards ye!" Granny was shouting. She drained a kettle of water onto the ground outside the door. Two boiled turnips remained in the pot. "Towards ye! Towards ye!"

Granny heard a small "puh" of ridicule from behind her. "You do be laughing at me back, Eamon, but the Wee Ones pass by at dawn and dusk. I'm afeared to plosh water on them without warning."

As if Eamon needed to hear this again. Granny used to say the same thing when she teemed the spuds. Watching her, he wondered if he'd dreamed the potato suppers she used to make, the way he'd dreamed the smell of roasted herring last month.

Potato stirabout, thickened with buttermilk. Dip-at-the-stool potatoes, topped with fresh fish dipped in salt.

And boxty—round potato cakes fried in pork fat—the boy's favorite. Tonight there was no stirabout, no buttermilk to kitchen the praties. Only skoddy.

When Granny set the pot on the flag of the hearth, Mamaí shuffled out of the back room, her once-lovely face long with grief. The family squatted around the pot like hares. Mamaí looked straight ahead at nothing, just as she always did. Hannah and Eamon stared into the pot. Two sliced turnips and a handful of oatmeal stared back.

"I hate skoddy," Hannah whimpered. "I hate turnips." Eamon passed the house spoon to his sister. She let it drop on the hard-packed clay floor.

"Oh, my sweetness," said Granny, "Father Gallagher brought these turnips last night. Himself probably went hungry so we could make a meal. And remember, this is New Year's Eve!"

When Granny's voice began to lilt, Eamon rolled his eyes, for he knew a faery tale was coming. "'Tis a great night for the Wee Ones' magic. I've a certain feeling they'll send your Uncle Jimmy from Kiltymore tomorrow. Hide and watch—he'll bring what we need to make relish cake."

Eamon let his shaggy black hair fall forward so Hannah couldn't see the disgust in his eyes. Relish cake was no treat at all. Just cattle blood fried with mushrooms and cabbage. Calamity food, he'd heard it called.

He dipped the tin spoon in the pot, added a pinch of salt, and held it to his sister's mouth. "Here now, Hannie. Just be trying this." Hannah squeezed her lips shut.

"Jimmy's coming?" asked Mamaí. Surprised, Eamon and Granny caught each other's eye. Since the sea had stolen Da, Mamaí never spoke or spun yarn or even knitted her shawls, which were much admired throughout the parish. Only her brother-in-law's name could loose the poor woman from her waking sleep.

Everyone in the parish loved Jimmy. Jimmy the Elbow, some called him, for the man had a strong bowing arm, he did, though he was lame of a leg. Just last winter, people had walked miles to hear him fiddle at Eamon's house, and a good spree it was. Da had taken the door off its hinges and set it on the floor, and throughout the night dancers cut the buckle to Jimmy's reels.

Most of Knockabeg was there, including Old Molly; the Widow Sweeney and her pretty daughter May; Margaret Carr, who lived on the hill above Eamon with her three strapping sons; the silly Campbell girls; the handsome schoolmaster, Samuel Love, and he always palavering at the ladies. Even Father Gallagher, who came to make sure the young people behaved themselves.

Not a hair was seen of Willaim Blaine and his wife on the night of the dance. This surprised no one. They were famous for staying home to stroke their shillings, do you see.

But there were no more dances after Da went out one morning in late March and rowed his canoe into a beardy white wave. When he never came up again, Jimmy was broken to bits. After his brother's funeral, he limped back to Kiltymore and seldom came to Knockabeg anymore.

"Aye," Granny said, "Jimmy *will* be here soon." Her eyes were bright with promise. "The faeries might even drop a pair of boots for Hannah down the chimney." The old woman pulled Hannah's big toe and winked.

Eamon frowned. "Granny, you shouldn't . . ."

"Why not? A faery may well take a fancy to our family. Last summer, I saw one flit over the lamb fold, clear as a star. Wore a spangled cape, she did."

Up on the roof, Sticky gasped. Granny had seen the Queen! Few mortals were innocent enough to possess the Sight — Sticky had never known a single one.

"Show me a faery," Eamon interrupted. "I wish to glory you would show me one!"

Granny made a sign of the cross over her chest and reached for her rosary hanging on the chimney wall. "Lord preserve us," she whispered.

Eamon felt anger curling out of his head and hands and feet, until it seemed to be altogether a separate person.

"Didn't I used to believe? After Da died, you said he'd gone to live with the Wee Ones. The devil be on me, you said, if faeries don't take care of drowned fishermen — that Da was living inside the hills with thousands of weeshy ladies and gentlemen. But you lied, Granny, you lied!"

On hearing the word *Da*, Mamaí pulled her shawl around her face and shuffled into the back room.

"Mamaí-e-e," Hannah wailed, but the poor widow knew only her own pain. Hannah ran over to the empty spinning wheel, stuck her thumb in her mouth, and sat with her face to the wall.

"Ah, now, and look what ye done," Granny said.

"Whatsomever." Shrugging, Eamon lifted the pot handles and went outside. As he threw the scraps of skoddy on the ground, he remembered how hopeful he'd been, looking for Da in the spring.

Granny had seemed so sure, you see! So, during April and May, when violets were blooming and cuckoos came back to the valley, Eamon made many a long trip up one side of Mully Mountain and down the other. He thrust his arms into every yellow gorse bush until his skin was raw with bramble cuts, for if one didn't have the doorway, wouldn't the next?

Alas, the lad never found a passage to a faery castle, and so he gave the go-bye to Granny's tale of hope. It's a fearful thing to lose trust in your elders and faeries at the same time.

Eamon let the wind carry this cruel memory and the skoddy away. *Father Gallagher is right,* he decided. *Faery talk is old talk and foolish talk.* So caught was he in this thought that seconds later, when a whiff of salty air tickled his nose, he smelled not a thing. And when a good deal of munching and lip-smacking commenced, the boy scarcely noticed his itching ears.

He closed the door and went in to face his grandmother. She and Hannah were lying in the outshot. Granny's hand rested on the child's tangled curls, her own hair a snow cap in the gloom.

Well now, she's asleep, Eamon thought, relieved the disagreement was over. He spread his straw on the floor and crawled under the threadbare blanket. Just as he closed his eyes, Granny spoke.

"Eamon, tomorrow we must eat petaties from the pit."

The boy knew he shouldn't argue. What was it Da used to say?—a silent mouth is sweet to hear. But only a few pounds of seed potatoes had been spared in the blight. These he had buried himself under a mound of straw, out in the field near the sunrise wall. Da had taught him to do just that when a crop failed.

"If we eat tomorrow, Granny, we starve next July!"

"How old are ye now, son?"

"Ten and so."

"Why then, is it striving to out-talk me you are, at your young age? Troth, you're a stubborn lad."

Granny turned silent again. A moment later, Eamon's two eyes were closed hard. Suddenly he heard a power of whacking snores that could raise a *pooka*. Or was it the tack-tok-tack of a tiny hammer on the roof?

Must be a faery, the boy thought. He snickered, then fell into a creamy potato dream.

That night, as hungry dreams held the people fast, a monster wind capered and cracked its fingers through the village lanes, like a wild creature dancing the jig. Only Sticky was awake to see it coming.

After listening to the debate below, the weeshy woman set to work. Twenty thorns from a haw bush were pinched between her lips, and a kit of tools hung around her neck. It had been a while since she'd made boots, but some faery skills, like learning to hop, are never forgotten.

Sticky rested her back against the chimney as she worked. "First, change bracken fern into leather," she reminded herself. "Cut, then stain with blossom juice from Blood-of-Christ bush. Sew pieces together with rose thorn needle. Hammer heel into sole with hawthorn nails. Polish with twelve drops of faery spit."

'Twas a ficklesome job, and she'd already broken two fingernails. Still, Sticky knew a pair of shoes would please Hannah, which would make Eamon smile, and wouldn't he grow the stronger for it? After all, she needed a solid boy, not a weakling.

Sticky was too busy to notice the rising wind, until a gust almost pushed her off the roof. When she looked up, she saw purple clouds building in the night sky — pillars that grew upward until they looked like cities entirely. Flocks of blackbirds flew in crazy figure eights, trapped between the columns of wind and rain.

The faery woman hugged the chimney and dug her heels into the thatch. While rain stung her face, she covered one ear. Turning the other to the east, she strained to listen. And what she heard gave her a heart-scalding.

"By this and by that!" Sticky cried out, "'Tis a faery battle. The war has begun!"

Indeed, somewhere far beyond the skies of Knockabeg, Trooping Faeries and Nuckelavees were joined in combat. Sticky thought of Mungo, fighting without her by her side.

And Wink — what was happening to him? He was ill prepared for violence — she hoped Jam was watching his back. After hearing a wail of wind that sounded like a cry of pain, Sticky tried to bury her shame and blame. "I'll warrant it's a cry of victory," she assured herself. "At this very moment, thousands of the beasties are probably dangling from sky nets."

The faery clung to the roof for several more hours, working on Hannah's boots. It wasn't easy. The skoddy she'd nibbled from the ground last night had made a thin supper. She was so hungry that she never noticed a lone six-inch creature flying over Eamon's field, and too tired to care when a gust of wind blew the cap from her head.

That's when the bla'guard William Blaine came out in a nightshirt to bring in some turf. What do ye think he saw? A bowlegged faery in a billowing red cloak, clutching Eamon's chimney.

"Saints of glory!" said Blaine, who never darkened the church door and couldn't have named a saint if Peter himself walked up and asked the time o'day. Blaine hurried into the house and told his wife, Red Sheila.

"Oxy, doxy, glorioxy!" the redhead replied. "I'd stake my life 'tis the self-same faery that stole our Frankie. All because you're too cheap to leave the Wee Ones a crust of bread!" Sheila then tried to brain her husband with a pot. Sure, and she blamed him for the stock of wood she'd found in her boy's bed last month instead of their lovely treasure of a son. "That faery has fixed her eye upon this house. Catch her or we'll sup sorrow for it!"

Blaine was so frightened by the thought of a faery curse that he took to his bed for the next two days. Now didn't that put Sheila in the foulest of moods? Neither of them bothered to check their field the next morning. Which proves that everyone, even rich folk, should respect a faery wind.

New Year's Day

When the inevitable sun began to rise, Sticky found her cap stuck in the chimney. She pulled it on and surveyed damage to the village. The straw on Blaine's potato pit was gone — young Frankie, you perceive, had done a lazy job of spreading it last spring. Now dozens of lumpers lay around Blaine's field. Eamon's pit was still safely covered, thank the saints above.

Sticky yawned. Oh, how she yearned for her rooms inside Mully Mountain! Yet it was clear from last night's argument that the family needed a day-watch, too, if Eamon were to survive. The boy was getting thinner every day. Somehow she had to make sure he ate the seed potatoes.

The faery clambered from one end of the roof to the other. "Should I move to the turf pile?" she wondered. "Too stuffy. The dung heap? Too smelly!"

Then she scanned Eamon's sloping yard. Halfway down the field was a spring tucked into the shoulder of a hedge bank. A stack of stones circled the spring, and a flat stone sat on top. From under it, Sticky would be safe from the sun's deadly rays, yet she could still keep Eamon in view.

"'Tis the very thing!" Sticky cried. Never one to waste time on decisions, she put Hannah's half-finished shoes in her tool kit and jumped over to the springhouse.

Once inside, she saw that some class of a faery had lived

there long ago and left the place a mess. Now it needed a woman's touch. A tapestry of clover perhaps, and a looking glass of polished quartz.

But first things first. Our Sticky had had a rough night of it, don't you see? Even faeries need naps.

"Well, then," she said, sighing. Thankful for the silence, the faery plucked an armful of spider webs from the ceiling. She spread them over her tired body and lay down for a nice sleep. Minutes later, a hard, dry ball of seaweed rolled down the bank and landed—ponk!—against the spring-house.

"Drat! Is there no rest for a weary faery?" Sticky looked out, and there, not ten squirrel lengths away, lay a clump of wriggling seaweed. Wrapped inside were hundreds of torn silver wings, a cabbage stump, and the saddest Trooping Faery eyes Sticky had ever seen.

"Whoever you be," she shouted, "take shelter or you'll turn to ashes!"

Sticky stuck one of her feet out in the sun to test its heat. Immediately the tip of her shoe began to smoke. "Curse this light!"

Horrified, she saw a sunbeam land directly on the sea-weed. "Unnhh," wept a voice within.

Forgetting herself entirely, Sticky threw her cape over her head and scuttled out to her comrade. Frantic, she pulled out an unrecognizable Wee One and wrapped it in her cape. "Oh my, oh my, oh my!"

Eyebrows aflame, Sticky managed to drag the bundle to the springhouse door and roll it inside. Sweat poured down her face as she ran straight to the trickle of spring water at the back. As her eyebrows sizzled, she finally saw the face of the faery she'd saved.

"Why, Wink," Sticky marveled, "'tis you." Aye, it was poor Wink, though he was too dart-shocked to answer. His wrist was broken, and the net had twisted his head, giving him a wry neck. Oddest of all, his hair had gone whiter than frosted grass. Now he looked like a shrunken old man.

When Sticky saw what Wink was wearing, she sank to the floor. Around his shoulders was a torn scarlet cloak, covered in dried blood. The lapel had been slashed just below an embroidered *M*, in the place where Mungo's heart would have been.

Sticky and Wink were most exhausted by their ordeal. Both faeries slept for hours, though Sticky had day-mares about Mungo's fate. Upon waking at dusk, she went outside and wished on a star for his safety.

She wished, too, that in course of time her eyebrows would grow back. Meanwhile her forehead was as bald as an egg stone, and she grimaced when she glanced in the mirror. She was not a lovely sight to look upon.

Still, show me a faery who's braver than Sticky, or kinder if it comes to that. Not forgetting that she had faults — she did, like any other faery — but Wink's great need seemed to bring out her noble side.

By midnight, she had made for him a bed of eagle feather pillows. She fashioned a cast from turnip leaves and rubbed in seal oil to set his wrist bone. Gratitude shone in

Wink's eyes, though he still couldn't speak, even after Sticky fed him Saint Mary's herb to cure the muteness.

Later that night, while a feathery snow fell outside, the two faeries lounged on the pillows. Happy to be in one piece, Wink hummed "King of the Faeries" as Sticky stitched the leather on one of Hannah's boots.

The sly faery woman knew it was easier to sing than to talk. "Wink, my friend, give us a song."

Wink's face turned red from the effort. "Nnnn!"

"We'll try together. Oh, the Faery King was a jolly old thing . . ."

"Nnnn . . . nnnn . . ."

"A jolly old thing was he . . . Wurra, I've pierced myself, right through the glove!"

Wink stared at the blood that dripped from Sticky's sheathed finger.

"Hunh . . . hunh . . . hunh." Two tears splashed down his cheeks with the memory that was on him. "We were . . ."

At last! thought Sticky. "Only when you're ready," she said.

Wink wiped his nose and cleared his throat. "We were fully prepared by Saint Stephen's Day. The Queen commanded the largest unit; the Steps headed up the others. Then last night we finally heard low calls of 'tattheration, tattheration.' What a sound . . ."

When Wink remembered that he'd wet his trousers, he lost his tongue again.

"Take your time," said Sticky.

The soldier breathed deeply, encouraged by her patience.

"We treaded air, waiting until the bogies bore down upon us. Hosts upon hosts of them. The men were so handsome, Sticky! Green satin capes, tall broad-brimmed hats.

"And the lovely women! Flowing hair, crowns of leaves. Dresses covered with foxglove blossoms, wings trimmed . . ."

". . . with silver," Sticky interrupted. "I don't need the fashion parade."

"Just as it seemed the Nuckelavees would overwhelm us, the Queen shouted 'Hie over cap!' We closed in so fast that they couldn't escape our nets. Herself's glasses fell off in the rush, and I lost my cape when I caught them. Still-in-all, thousands of the beasts lost their wings and dropped straight into the sea."

Where they will make storms, Sticky thought bitterly, *just to see mortals drown.*

"After winning that first round, we rested on a cloud. Jam thought we should come home. I advised the Queen, and quite wisely, I must say, that Nuckelavees don't give up so easily."

Actually, it was Wink who had wanted to come home, but aren't faeries the worst ones for telling a cockeyed tale?

Sticky was almost afraid to ask. "Mungo?"

Wink's lower lip hung down. "The Queen sent Mungo on a scouting mission. Only his horse returned . . . with the cape tied to its tail. She gave it to me for safekeeping."

Sticky lifted Mungo's cape from a twig peg on the wall. She put her fingers through the slash and rubbed the *M*.

"With no warning the Nuckelavees attacked again. Some of us were able to quickly organize our nets and darts, but this time the curs were armed with grass blades every bit as sharp as clam shells. The blood of many Trooping Faeries stained the ocean last night."

"What of Frankie Blaine? Was he no help at all?"

"That cowardly boy! At first sight of a grass blade, he dropped his corner of the net. And wasn't I flying just beneath it? When the other net holders let go, I was trapped in the seaweed. As I fell through the thunderheads I spied you in the distance on Eamon's roof. I tried to steer the horse toward the cabin, but I guess I fainted."

"And you broke your wrist when you landed."

Wink nodded and massaged his belly. He looked most worn out. "I'm hungry. Would there be a certain thing as a potato on Granny's windowsill?"

Sticky threw a spider web over him. "Rest now. I'm after dropping Hannah's boots down the chimney. At day-stir I'll return for a wee nap."

She had not the heart to tell Wink the bad news: there were no decent eatables left within the walls of Eamon's house.

I'm sure I'm within the truth when I say there's nothing sweeter than a little girl with a new pair of shoes. Nothing noisier, either. The next morning, Sticky awoke to Hannah's squeals.

The faery woman threw off her spider webs and pulled a

dart from her pocket. "Will I never get a decent bit of rest?" she raged. "A shot in the girl's hind parts might quiet her down."

Standing as close to the opening of the springhouse as she dared, for the sun was fully risen, Sticky took aim. When she saw the scene in the cottage yard, she dropped her hand. *"Ach,* I cannot do it."

Indeed, the shoes had made the family forget their hunger and care for a time. Jimmy, awakened during the night by the storm, had arrived at dawn, just as Granny predicted.

Now he was sitting on a boulder, drawing a few lively notes from his fiddle. On his head was a floppy felt hat, and though his greatcoat was patched, he wore it as proudly as a cock, for the man had a self-respecting way about him.

Hannah spun up and down the sloping yard to the music. "Look, Eamon! Eamon, look!" Every few seconds, the child stopped to swipe dust from the shoe tops, she was that proud of them.

Why, then, thought Sticky, pleased with her handiwork. *Doesn't she look like a dancing dolly?*

Eamon rested on a little turf stack that stood thatched with rushes before the door. He smiled secretly at his uncle. Sure, it was Jimmy who had stolen the shoes from Blaine's store, then put them in the fireplace before waking the family. Not that Eamon would have risked his soul to take the shoes himself, you understand.

Jimmy winked. "Well, Eamon. You're a fine one for

looking after your sister." Jimmy, don't you see, was certain his nephew had filched the boots.

Mamaí and Granny huddled on a bench by the door in the rare winter sun. Both were wrapped head to knee in Mamaí's knitted black shawls. The mother nodded as Hannah danced, and for once, her eyes looked as if she were living in this world and not the other.

Granny was nodding, too. The old woman wouldn't say "I told you so" to Eamon about faery magic, but she might think it — yes, she might.

"Son, did you bring the blood?" she asked Jimmy.

"Ah, and so I did. It's here in me sack, along with a nice fat cabbage." Jimmy opened the sack and pulled out a noggin of cow's blood. A rag was stuffed into the top of the wooden jar.

"Fresh as daisies." He laid the cabbage and the noggin in Granny's hands. "I cut the cow meself just before dawn."

Eamon chewed his lip and looked at the bloody rag. In spite of his rolling stomach, he was curious. "Did the cow die then?"

"No, no, not a bit of it. You cut a vein in the neck and take a few pints, see." Jimmy flourished his fiddle bow in the air as if it were a knife. "Next, slap on a few hairs from the tail to stop the bleeding. Then close the slit with a pin. Old Bridey balked some, but she'll be right soon enough."

"Old Bridey!" Granny cried. "You bled Lord Shank's fattest cow? Jimmy, Jimmy, listen to me now, for an old broom knows the dirty corners best. It's two months late you are on the rent. You'd best not bring the landlord's bad heart upon yourself."

Jimmy laughed. He was devil-may-care when it came to Shank. "Oh, now, I only borrowed a little blood from the lordy Lord."

Eamon laughed, too, for he loved to hear his uncle make sport of the landlord. The boy passed the estate house every time he went to market in Kiltymore. With its two wings, four chimneys, and twenty-four windows, it seemed to Eamon the grandest building in the world. Once he had asked Da if Shank and his wife were virtuous people to deserve such riches.

"Do not mistake a goat's beard," Da had said with a scowl, "for a fine stallion's tail."

As Jimmy pulled a long face that looked like the lord himself, Granny fingered the cabbage in her lap. Mind, she was hungrier than a bird. Only the greatest sense of dignity kept her from peeling the raw leaves and stuffing them into her mouth.

"You're worse than Eamon for the arguing," she told Jimmy. "Now go in and rake the fire for the relish cake. Eamon, there be mushrooms growing under the bridge. Will ye come with me to fetch them?"

But when Granny stood up, she swayed like a drunk at a wedding. If Mamaí hadn't grabbed her elbow, the old woman would have fallen to the ground.

Hannah's eyes turned darker than old tea with the fear that was in them. "Granny, are ye sick?"

"Hush, my jewel, I'm well enough."

Still leaning against Mamaí, Granny looked at Eamon. Her face was the color of tallow. "Eamon, the petatie pit . . ."

Eamon shook his head and started toward the pit. "Da wouldn't like a bit of this."

Usually the boy made a wide circle around the spring-house, for Granny insisted on it. "I hear Wee Ones lived there long ago," she often said. "You should respect a place that has the name of being gentle."

This day, Eamon was too worried to care. He marched straight past the springhouse, near enough to enter its shadow. So close that a weensy hand could dart out and squeeze his right leg, for the testing of the strength in it, though Sticky well knew that a faery's touch would leave a bruise upon his flesh.

On reaching the pit, Eamon fell to his knees and pulled off the straw. Moments later his body began to shake.

"Oh, God in heaven!" the boy prayed. He dug deeper and deeper, but every potato looked the same — shriveled and black as bog water. The stink of them filled the air until even Sticky, twenty perches away in the springhouse, gagged.

Eamon threw himself across the rotten mound. "Da, Da, what on the living earth will we do at all? These tatties have turned black, too!"

Sticky smacked the top of her head. "Look in Blaine's field, you senseless, worthless worm of a boy!" she shouted. "His lumpers are all about!"

Eamon felt a powerful prickle in his left ear, and even a boy in a raving fit of tears has to scratch himself. The louder

Sticky yelled, the more he itched, as if a caterpillar were crawling through his head.

Why, you've never seen the likes of it — a scrawny lad dancing wildly around a field with a finger in his ear. At last he landed against Blaine's wall, spied the potatoes on the other side, and . . . well, now you know what the family had for supper that night, and sure, they ate with a heart and a half. It's true what the people say: hunger does make a good sauce.

Saint Brigid's Eve

Who amongst us can measure the pain of starvation? The hungry are too weak to tell of it. The well-fed are too comfortable to imagine it. But two faeries knew, they did indeed.

One month later, Wink and Sticky were suffering as deeply as any mortal. 'Twas the bitter cold eve of Saint Brigid's Day, when farmers honored their special saint. That night Sticky returned from the cabin with empty hands.

"Was there nothing for us on the windowsill?" Wink asked.

"Not a wafer of Blaine's potatoes are left. And the cabin shows no sign of preparation for Saint Brigid — no cross over the door to bring good luck, nor any in the field. What's worse, Jimmy has joined the household. The man couldn't pay his rent, so yesterday Shank sent Red Coats with guns to Kiltymore. The soldiers threw Jimmy out of his cottage and barred the door."

"Whisht! Isn't that a burning shame!"

"Aye, and it means one more mouth to feed. Mamaí cries all day by reason of her gums bleeding. Hannah's arms and legs are coming in crooked — I fear she'll be crippled soon."

"The boy?"

Sticky rubbed her hands, as if the gloves were too tight. "It's bad with him. He's not grown the length of a snail. And Granny can't get out of bed at all, her joints are that swollen. The Queen was right, Wink. The mortals of Knockabeg may starve."

"Sticky," Wink said shyly. "I've wanted to ask for ever so long. Why do you wear the gloves? And why did you desert the Queen?"

Isn't a secret the heaviest load? Sticky looked as if she longed to answer. "I think I'll check the windowsill again," she said instead. "Maybe the priest has brought a bite of food."

The faery went out the door and into a blizzard of sideways snow. "The devil have ye!" she cursed. As she hopped to the house, it seemed to her that the hills of Knockabeg held all the sorrows of the world. Was there ever such a heartsick place, with its falling rain and snow and tears?

There was a place as sorrowful as Knockabeg, for the Solitary Ones had ruined its beauty long ago. Beyond West Isle, across the channel, and on the coast of East Isle squatted a smoky city. In this filthy town was a factory. It ran on coal and the heart's blood of humans worked half to death. And in the gut of the factory's smokestack, on the Prisoner's Ledge, lay Mungo.

Mungo was not alone in the smokestack, for the shaft was home nest for most Solitary Ones. The clever creatures had built ledges up and down the dark tube. Some of these were offices; others were sleeping cells. Each was veiled with a curtain of soot, so the occupants could rest in isolation.

'Twas here that the Solitary Ones returned after nights of wicked play. The despair of the factory below was their sleeping tonic, the sound of grinding machinery a soothing lullaby.

The Chief resided on the topmost ledge, near the mouth of the stack. As luck would have it, Mungo was directly below. Escape was impossible.

The Chief, you perceive, was a Dallahan who carried his severed head in his right hand. In his left he cracked a whip made of a human spine. When the dark man held his head aloft, he could see everything in the tower at once, even if the factory burped up a plume of smoke. No faery, especially a prisoner, left or entered the bunker without the Chief's permission.

On Saint Brigid's Eve, Mungo was in despair. Small blame to him! Since a sniper had caught him spying over the mouth of the smokestack, the Trooping Faery had been most kilt with the pain from his punctured chest. A smear of faery ointment was all that was needed. But Mungo's guards brought him nothing of the sort — only an occasional piece of rancid kidney pie stolen from a lunch bucket in the factory below.

Wouldn't it be easier to give up? Mungo wondered as he nibbled a crumb of pie crust. He was wishing only for a good giggle with Sticky and a comfortable retirement back in Knockabeg, when a horde of Solitary Ones swarmed up to see the Chief.

All the bogey-beasts the Queen had mentioned now hovered in line by Mungo's ledge: a clump of Sheerie needing their corpse-lights rekindled; three Mermen who demanded that their long teeth be sharpened; a Gray Man wanting a fog replacement so he could cause shipwrecks. Last was a tiny Nuckelavee named Nigel who lacked a wing.

"Move along!" Nigel snarled. "Bad enough to lose a wing to those Trooping Ones last month. Now I have to wait behind you stupid knaves?"

Trooping Ones! Behind his curtain of soot, Mungo kept perfectly still, hoping to hear news of his clan.

One of the Merfolk turned around and puckered his snout at Nigel. "Shut yer gob, midget, or I'll give ye a smack!" When the other Mermen laughed, their scaly faces cracked. Flakes of skin drifted over to Mungo's ledge and landed in his nostrils. He tried not to sneeze.

"Nigel, did you crush out all them Trooping Faeries?" asked the Gray Man.

"Nah, a few survived."

Ho, Mungo thought, *and that's welcome news.*

"I managed to break through enemy lines and hit a few potato pits. We'll lay a curse on others in the next attack."

"And when is that?" shrilled a Sheerie.

"May Eve, after the snows of winter have passed. One more assault in midsummer should destroy the new crop, and we'll have West Isle humans where we want them."

Begob, thought Mungo, *these Nuckelavees are fiends!*

Nigel's remaining gossamer wing shook with anticipation. "Mortals who don't starve right off will soon be killing one another for food. Then the wickedness will be complete. We can bring a supply of kidney pie, move in, and colonize the island. Be nice to get out of this dump, eh?"

With that, a great puff of smoke curled up the chimney and stopped the conversation. Mungo coughed and waited for the fumes to pass. The news of surviving Trooping Ones gave him hope, and now he considered his choices. Well, there was but one, if you go to that. He had to get word to the Queen about the next assault.

Every morning the sun passed directly over the opening of the smokestack. Mungo knew that during those brief dangerous moments, the Dallahan held his head behind his back. If the wounded faery could gather his strength, this would be the time to leap up and out to freedom.

But how to save himself from the sun? And could he stand the pain of the jump? Mungo had much to ponder as Solitary Ones flew up and down the shaft, their voices like locusts in his ears, so. As he lay in a tremble of fear, all courage left him. For is it not in the darkest hours of night when hope seems farthest away?

Saint Brigid's Day

Much sooner than Mungo expected, light appeared over the mouth of the smokestack. *Death-alive, it's time,* he quaked.

On seeing the fatal rays, the Dallahan turned his ugly head backwards and thrust it between his knees. There was not a moment to waste. Mungo stuck a thumb in his chest wound, took a deep breath, and bent his elbows. Just before making the leap, he looked up to aim himself.

Heigh ho! he thought. *I* am *seeing the sun, amn't I? It looks ever so much like a torch!*

A familiar voice ricocheted off the circular wall of the shaft. "Jump now, Mungo, jump!"

The confused Dallahan snorted. Just a second too late, he held up his head and swiveled it around the smokestack. Eyes the color of pus followed Jam's voice up to the opening. When they saw a Trooping Faery balanced on the rim, flames shot from the head's nose.

"That's no sun!" Mungo cried. "'Tis Jam with a blazing stick o' bog fir!" Mungo was off like a shot, with the Solitary Ones setting off hotfoot after him. A jumble of images streaked by—dripping yellow eyes, a zipping whip, fingers that reached for his flying body.

"Vengeance!" the Dallahan howled. "Vengeance!"

But Mungo went from the Chief's sight like a shred of

mist. As he reached the top, Jam stretched out both hands to pull him clear of the opening. While grass blades rained around them, the two soldiers jumped on Jam's horse, Mungo riding on the back.

The horse bucked and bounced through the foul East Isle night. At last the faery men could breathe deeply of clean ocean air, and after a time, they entered the quiet of a cloud.

"Devil fly away with you, Mungo, but you're a great trouble," Jam complained. "Haven't I looked down every grimy East Isle smokestack since you disappeared?"

"Ah, and I'm begging your pardon."

Jam wiggled his earlobes, a sure sign of faery anger. "Well, it wasn't my idea. I had orders from the Queen. With Wink missing in action, I thought I should stay by her side. But Her Honor said she couldn't bear to lose two Steps, so there you have it."

"Wink is gone?" Truth to tell, Mungo had always thought Wink a bit of a plodder. Now, to his surprise, he felt a thorn of grief in his throat.

"This is why my orders are twofold. The Queen says she needs a better mortal boy. That crybaby Frankie Blaine keeps calling for his mother, you see. Doesn't have the blood of a hen in him. So you and I are to fly to Knockabeg and bring Sticky's lad to Frog Leg Island."

Mungo's heart broke for Sticky. He had never seen a faery so intent on guarding a mortal. What on the wide earth was there for her except the boy-o? Well, she wouldn't give him up easily. He must give her time to get used to the idea.

"Never mind Frankie now," said Mungo. "I've news of the next attack. The Queen should hear it straight away so the troops can prepare." After a great gob of faery chatter, Mungo finally convinced Jam to drop him off in Knockabeg, where he could recover from his wound. Jam would fly directly to the Queen with Mungo's report. Then Mungo himself would deliver Eamon in time for the battle eight weeks hence.

This settled, the two soldiers rode all night and reached the tweedish mountains of Knockabeg shortly before dawn. As they descended through a fistful of cloud, Mungo looked very keenly at the scene below. "Ah, the undecent faeries who've brought this upon the people! I'll give that Nigel a good drubbing before it's over!"

Piles of blackened potatoes lay neatly in almost every field. Twenty new crosses stood in the churchyard cemetery. Lines of mortals from all directions were plodding toward the crossroads — farmers with empty buckets, mothers with baskets, children with piggins.

"I'm surprised they're not in church on this holy day," said Jam. "Isn't Saint Brigid the patron saint of farmers?"

"Slih, slih . . . she's of no help to them now." Mungo narrowed his eyes at the ragged bunch below. "I see Eamon's *mamaí*. And is that his Uncle Jimmy? They must be going to Blaine's."

As the horse landed by the tower, the faeries heard low words on the wind:

"Oh, Granny the beloved, Granny the beloved, fair woman of our heart — are ye dead? Are ye dead?"

"By jingo," Jam said, "I'd swear 'tis a Banshee's call!"

And I'd swear 'tis Sticky, thought Mungo.

He hopped off and slapped the horse's rear. "Off with you, Jam! Tell Herself I'll bring the boy by May Eve. She has my word."

Mungo watched Jam's horse rise and cut through the mist. Then he followed the wail through the fields and along the creek until it led him to Eamon's house. The faery noticed that the thatch on the roof had turned black and in some places was sinking with rot. The yard was untidy and puddled with filth.

"Ochón! Ochón!" Mungo threw his eye from the roof to the door to the dung heap. Where was the husky voice he knew so well?

A soggy sun was about to rise. Mungo slipped quickly through the cottage wall to protect himself, but once inside, the faery man found such misery that he wished he'd never escaped from East Isle at all, at all.

Mungo smelled Granny before he saw her. Though he clapped both hands to his mouth and nose, the stench of the woman's soiled straw choked him. "God of glory be about me. Have I fallen to Under-the-Ground?"

The spark o'fire in the grate was nearly dead, and a chill sat on the air. A pot of cold mush rested by the hearth. Granny lay in her outshot, so thin that the bones rolled under her skin. Her lips were cracked and bleeding. "Water . . . a mouthful of water."

"It's here, Granny," Eamon said. He knelt by her side

and held a piggin to her mouth with shaking hands. Granny's arms waved aimlessly over her chest like broken wings. Standing on tiptoe in her scuffed boots, Hannah reached up and tried to still the old woman's gnarled fingers. "Be still now, Granny. You do be scaring me!"

"She can't help it," Eamon said hoarsely.

"Ochón! Ochón!"

Hannah jumped. "Eamon, someone's wailing again! Can ye hear it?"

"No, Hannie, ye be dreaming. Fetch us more water, will you?"

But Mungo had heard it. He turned toward the sound and glimpsed a snatch of red satin between the closed dresser doors. When the children's heads were turned, he put his finger in the pull-hole and slowly opened the doors. "Ah, here you are," he whispered.

Sticky sat on the top shelf, combing her short hair with a great fury as if that would make it longer. So overcome was she by the sight of her old friend that she buried her face in his shoulder. "Where have you . . . ? *Ach,* there's a hole in your vest . . . Do ye need a poultice . . . ? Granny is drawing near to her last account . . . What if Eamon goes next?"

Embarrassed, Mungo patted her arm. "Yes, yes, now. Hush, hush. Maybe Jimmy and Mamaí will bring back the meal in time. I saw them going to Blaine's store." Not that Mungo had a pinpoint of trust in the storekeeper, but some words are best left tucked under the tongue.

"You may well say so, but 'tis Blaine's meal that's killing

them! He's been selling some strange, foreign corn. The stuff is coarse, and Mamaí doesn't cook it long enough. It runs like mud through the mortals' bodies."

Just then, Granny cried out. Mungo and Sticky peeked through the pull-hole and grew quiet, for the cramping that squeezed Granny's swollen stomach was most awful to watch. After a time, the old woman's breathing slowed. Finally, she gave one last sigh.

"Granny's gone," Eamon said quietly. He opened the door so her spirit could leave the house, then looked about the cottage with vacant eyes. The boy wanted only to think of salmon jumping in the creek, or the dance of violets on the hills, or gannets that swooped by when he fished from the cliffs. Anything but death.

Hannah pulled on her brother's ragged shirttail. "Where, Eamon? Where is Granny gone?"

On seeing the stricken look on his sister's face, Eamon couldn't help himself. He knelt down, looked Hannah full in the eye, and prayed his falsehood would be forgiven. "When Father Gallagher buries Granny beneath the sod, he'll say God has her soul. But I can tell you in all certainty that the faeries have her now."

Inside the dresser, Sticky nodded. *Aye, the good woman had faith in us,* she thought, *and the Sight, too. Granny has died before her natural time. She deserves every Wee One's hospitality.*

"Oh, that's all right then," said Hannah. Contented, she went over to her mother's empty spinning wheel. "I'll just be spinning yarn so Mamaí can make a shawl." Mamaí had not knitted an inch since Da died, but isn't the pretending of a small child a grand thing?

Eamon's voice cracked. "Ah, Hannie, that would be lovely." With a groan, he picked up Granny's thin corpse and tenderly carried it back to the cow byre, where Mamaí and Margaret Carr would clean it as best they could, there being no oat seed left in the house to wash with.

"Take care, Eamon," Sticky warned softly. "I don't need a boy with a strained back!"

When her brother left the room, Hannah dragged the creepy to the outshot. Her little elbows poking out like sticks, she struggled to lift herself into the dirty straw. The child nestled into the shape left by Granny's form, then fell asleep.

For a long while all was still within the dresser and the cold house. After a time, Mamaí and Jimmy came up the slope with empty noggins. Both had a wretched cast to their cheeks. When Jimmy saw his mother's body in the byre, he hurled his noggin against the wall, and had Eamon not stopped him, the crazed man would have smashed his fiddle, too.

"The devil take Blaine and his missus," Jimmy cried, "for not giving us one shilling of credit. May their son, and his sons, and all their sons, turn into blooming eejits!"

While Jimmy laid this curse on the meal man, Mamaí began to keen. *"Ochón, ochón!"*

Her wail was soon joined by a whispered lament from

the dresser. The sounds of grief joined together and floated toward the heavens, where perhaps someone was listening.

Nay, a light heart would not be found in that cabin for many a day.

So. By light-most-gone, the family lay a'weary by the hearth, and Sticky's eyes were red as a radish. Mungo laid a firm hand on her shoulder. "You'll be no good to the boy without a rest."

With a last anxious look at Eamon, Sticky led Mungo to the springhouse. There he found his cape hanging on the wall and Wink flopped on the pillows, and you may set it down that both reunions gave him an equal measure of joy. While Sticky boiled dandelion roots to bring down the swelling on Mungo's wound, he and Wink got quite thick entirely.

"What gumption!" Mungo said when Wink told him about his broken wrist.

"May I never stir, but that's luck!" cried Wink on hearing of the wicked Nigel and of Mungo's rescue.

As Mungo described the smokestack, he marched up and down, his cape swinging behind him. The garment did rest well upon his shoulders. It seemed to give him more wisdom than ever, and the Lord be thanked for that. In them times in Knockabeg, wisdom was scarce as food. Oh, the things that be happening after Granny's death!

The next week, Widow Sweeney crumpled on the road while walking to Blaine's store. Old Molly went into the clay soon after. Then one day there were too many bodies and not enough coffins. When the youngest Campbell girl died, the priest rolled her into the grave in a linen winding-sheet — the only one left in the village. The families shared this shroud and whatever else they had, and gladly, too.

Except Margaret Carr's sons. Since autumn, they had hoarded a chest of oats and a sack of seed potatoes for spring planting. Mistrustful of starving neighbors, the young men sowed half of the seeds in their ridgy field and sold the rest to buy a musket.

Margaret wept in her apron to think it had come to this. Yet she did not stay their hands when they pointed the gun at Eamon's house. Nor did the neighbors receive a particle of her oaten bread.

Lord Shank finally took pity on the hungry cotters in March. He hired the poorest of them so they could buy Blaine's meal, but didn't they have to slave for it! Every morning Eamon's family and scores of others walked six miles to build a road up the glen — a famine road, the people still call it. Shank's guards carried whips, and the pay was only one turnip and ten pence a day.

Because Jimmy was lame, he had a tough task of hauling the stones. One cold, wet afternoon, a guard fired him without pay, and that night in the cottage, the fiddler composed a lament he named "Lord Shank." Clear as water, the notes were. They streamed down Knockabeg's lanes and seeped into the cabins, where both living and dying were soothered by the sound.

The next morning, Jimmy awoke before the family. From the dresser, Sticky watched him pack his fiddle. Silently he crept from the cabin, limping toward the open road. She returned to the springhouse in a most dreary state of mind. "What will the family do now?" she brooded. "I fear Eamon's uncle has left to become a beggar."

"Begging will go hard with Jimmy," Mungo observed. "It kills a proud man sooner than hunger—I'll wager he doesn't return."

Toward the middle of April, three red-coated soldiers with muskets and the gr-r-reat Lord Shank rode into Knockabeg. A wagon rolled behind them, loaded with sacks of barley meal, peas, and beans. In the back sat a forty-gallon kettle big enough for Lady Shank to bathe in.

Mungo heard the procession tramp across the bridge. "Wurra! Shank is setting up a soup kitchen!"

"Soup for us?" bleated Wink. The poor fellow had lain on the pillows for hours, he was that listless.

Sticky shook her finger in his face. "Of course not, you half-witted dolt!" Who cared about Wink when her future wandered the yard, his young life draining away?

"Sticky, what's the use of spiteful words?" Mungo said. "A mortal might well leave us a sip of broth."

"She's always been dark against me," blubbered Wink, whose hunger had made him forget Sticky's kindness during his recovery. "Ballyragging a faery for having the hope of food in him!"

Someone has to be the peacemaker in difficult times. So

it was Mungo who called an emergency High Council meeting that night. At dark-half-gone, the threesome left for the tower by the cliff. It seemed a great trouble to go this far, but Mungo knew the ancient meeting place would lend weight to his words, and he had much to say.

Rain squalls were rolling in from the sea. Mungo, skinny as a sand eel and still sore from his wound, hauled Wink on his back. Sticky followed, arms crossed and legs more bowed than ever. An unhappier creature you never saw.

The faeries settled themselves against the cairn and touched knees. "May Eve is drawing near," Mungo said over the whipping wind.

Sticky's voice was sharper than nettles. "What of it?"

Patiently, Mungo explained the Nuckelavees' plan to attack Frog Leg Island on May Day. Avoiding Sticky's eyes, he saved the worst for last: his promise to bring Eamon to the Queen.

Sticky shook her fist in Mungo's face. "You'll not have him."

"If you truly cared about the lad, you'd *want* me to take him. Jam said Frankie Blaine is good for stealing the food, even if he is gutless in a fight. Surely there's more to eat on Frog Leg than here."

"But since Granny's death, Mamaí rocks and prays all day. Hannie might as well be an orphan. She's a fragile child, and too young to lose her brother so soon!"

Ah, so it's "Hannie" now, thought Mungo. Sticky's switch to the tender nickname could mean only one thing. "I know

65

a way to keep the boy and his family alive. But when it's time, you must let him go with me."

Sticky's eyes were wild with worry. "You'll return him?"

Mungo shivered as he remembered the wingless Nigel. The faery had little hope that Eamon would live to see Knockabeg again. "After the battle," he promised.

"Another battle?" whimpered Wink. The war-weary faery tumbled over into a ball. *Ach,* the blood and pain of combat had given him more imagination than ever he would need.

"Wink, no one expects you to fight without your cape. You and Sticky will stay here to help the family. *If* you can get along." Throwing a keen look at Sticky, Mungo rolled Wink to a sitting position.

"Now then, here is the plan." They would need a perfectly round black pebble, Mungo said, and a set of faery harp strings. "Above all," he reminded them, "hold on to your caps — we must stay invisible."

The faery warrior gave orders as if he were the Queen, which, of course, he was not, but necessity required that he act the part. At least that's the way I got the grasp of the thing. And before long, the three pranksters, even Sticky, were awash in giggles as they planned their lovely trick.

By the heavens above me, I wish you could have been at William Blaine's store the next day. There is many an old person still about Knockabeg who minds it well. To begin with, the best way to keep loyalty in a man's heart is to keep money in his purse. Shank paid Blaine to take charge of the soup, so Blaine helped the Lord's favorites first and gave them the most. Father Gallagher tried to supervise, but Blaine's ladle was too quick for him entirely.

Now you take the schoolmaster, Samuel Love. He'd always bowed deeply when Lady Shank's carriage passed the schoolhouse. And look here, didn't Love get a slopping noggin of soup, plus a generous helping of barley from the bottom of the pot!

Eamon, howsomever, waited hours for a scant piggin's worth, and the thinnest part at that. Behind him a tired Hannah leaned against her mother's legs. Every few moments, Mamaí crossed herself, she was that cracked with the religion. They were a forlorn group, but Blaine shorted them anyway, just for being Jimmy's relations.

By midday, when the clouds were so dark that imps could roam safely about, Blaine's missus came running out of her house, headed toward the crossroads.

"William," Red Sheila cried on reaching the store, "there's a faery pebble in the teakettle! The water's asleep and won't boil at all! Come home this instant, I tell ye!"

Blaine was most afeared to touch a faery stone, but he wasn't after getting hit with Sheila's pot lid, either. The meal man threw a horseshoe beside the soup kettle to protect it from a faery raid. Shedding his apron, he rushed after his wife.

"Do be watching the soup for me," Blaine called back to Father Gallagher. "I won't be long."

The couple took a shortcut across the bog, and what did they do but tread upon a bewitched sod of grass! Soon they were lost, even with the cabin in plain sight. Ninety steps forward they took, yet the house was no closer than when they left. 'Twas as if invisible strings were keeping them back.

Now, what do you make of that? I've never been able to account for it meself. Around in circles they went, until the missus was pulling out her red hair and Blaine stood almost drowned in a bog sink.

As this went forward, people at the store filled their noggins. Greedily they slurped the soup, then lined up again. The priest supervised, so all was done with fairness. Everyone left with enough for supper, and by my soul, they did give thanks for the watery stuff.

That night William and Sheila crawled into bed with the chill, whilst Eamon and his kin went to bed with their hunger eased. The boy and Mamaí instantly fell asleep, but Hannah lay awake in the outshot, wishing for Granny. The child missed the old woman most at night when the cabin was pot-black, for there was no turf left at all, you see.

A pair of gold-speckled hands suddenly appeared in the darkness. Hannah opened her eyes wide and sat up on her elbows. *'Tis a faery!* she thought.

One shiny hand spread itself wide open. From pinky to thumb, it moved down the length of Eamon's sleeping form, as if to measure him. The hands floated to the hearth, hesitated, and went back to pat the boy's head. After a time, they slowly disappeared up the chimney.

Hannah gurgled with delight. How well she remembered what Granny used to do! She filled a piggin with leftover soup and lifted the window. And before she could say "God bless," ten gleaming fingers snatched the cup from the sill and disappeared.

"Ptuui!" Wink took a sip of soup from his acorn and spat it out. "So it's feet-washing water, is it?"

Mungo tried not to whine. "'Tis a strange mixture right enough. Not a bean in sight."

"Amn't I the lucky one?" Sticky said. She lifted a pod from her acorn and wrinkled her nose. "Here's the one pea in the lot."

"Share! Share!" Wink demanded. He thrust his acorn toward Sticky, who rolled her eyes but obliged. Using her needle, she sliced the pea into three parts.

Quite ravenous, Mungo swallowed the morsel whole and wiped his mouth. "This will never do at all," he declared. "The family needs animal flesh, as do we."

Once again the trio gathered in a circle, knees and caps touching. The only sound in the springhouse was the tinkle of cap bells and water dripping from the back wall. I'll tell ye, despite the spats that starvation was bringing upon them, they made a fine team, they did.

Before night was over, Sticky had searched the shallows for every shellfish left by the tide. She insisted on doing it alone, and perhaps that was best. You wouldn't have wanted to hear her curses in regard to the Nuckelavees.

"By my tongue, I'll get even with them yet," she ranted as she gathered mussels and limpets. "Six horseloads of manure upon the brutes!"

Sticky stashed the fishies under a rock on a stretch of shore where Eamon often wandered. With the help of another fit of itching, the lad found them in the morning, before other hungry souls stripped the sand of sea life altogether.

While Sticky gathered her bits of food, Mungo wove a rope of sea grass for Wink, then knotted his cape into a rucksack. The partners hastened to the steep cliffs above the sea to search for gulls' eggs.

'Twas dangerous business, but no hurling mates ever worked better or with more trust. As Wink held the rope, Mungo bounced from crag to crag, and by night-most-gone, his rucksack overflowed with eggs.

Well, that was the way it went for the next few weeks. The faeries gathered carrageen seaweed, which makes a meal when boiled, if not a toothsome one. Along hidden faery paths, they found pig nuts and bog berries. Using spiders as bait, they trapped baby frogs. They even dredged the creek for the wormy larva of beetles.

Each morning, Eamon roamed restlessly around the yard, scratching his feet until he came upon the wee piles of food. These were barely enough to feed faeries, much less Eamon's family. Still, by the end of April, all within the cabin and springhouse were still alive.

There are those who would say 'twas a miracle. I cannot tell ye the truth of the matter, as one must rely on faith to believe such.

May Eve

It's common faery fact that moon fall is the best time for stealing a child . . . after the moon leaves but before dawn arrives. For troubled mortals who cannot sleep, this is the dark time. It tugs on the soul and never seems to end.

For Sticky, in the early hours of May Eve, the moments were passing all too fast. "Mungo, can ye not wait until cock crow?" she begged.

Mungo was in no mood for an argument. He piled two flat stones on the springhouse floor, placed his cape between them, and hopped on top. "Eamon will be wanting a sturdy breakfast on Frog Leg."

The faery warrior jumped up and down. "And the lad needs a full day of training." Mungo took his cape out of the press and examined it closely. Confidence in battle is everything, do you see. Only the crispest of pleats will do.

"What class of a breakfast do ye suppose there'll be on the island?" Wink asked in a thin voice.

"Oh, all kinds of important eating and drinking. Fresh eggs, rashers of bacon, potato stirabout, buttermilk galore."

The boy would have only war rations of dried herring, but Mungo hoped the promise of hearty food for Eamon would comfort Sticky. Instead, she moved to the back of the springhouse and pouted.

Mungo panicked. Aroo! Was she planning another trip

to Devil's Rock? "You have to cooperate, Sticky! Everyone's survival — mortal and faery alike — depends on Eamon!"

"What about me? What of *my* survival?"

"Do you hear that, Mungo?" Wink squeaked. "Her self-ishness is higher than Mully Mountain."

Sticky glowered at Wink. "You know nothing about me."

"I know you'll never get back to Above-the-Sky."

The faery woman's jaw dropped. "Why, you miserable little grub . . ."

"I'm sure I'm right, Sticky," shrilled Mungo, "when I say there's no bearing you at all! If we know nothing about you, how can we understand you?"

Sticky turned most rampageous. "All right," she flared, "all right! But do you vow to keep quiet about it? If the Queen finds out, she'll think I'm a spy."

"I swear."

"Tell, tell!" said Wink, who'd got his ears up at the promise of juicy gossip.

Sticky paced the room like a trapped weasel. "I hardly know how to begin. You both think I'm a *Deenee Shee*, but you're wrong. I'm a Solitary One."

"Blatherskite," Mungo protested, for it's hard to admit we never know our friends as well as we might.

"Not all of us are wicked," Sticky was quick to explain. "A few, like Banshees, are kind. They live on their own and avoid the evil ones. Leprechauns are harmless, too. My first post was as apprentice to one of them."

"A shoemaker?" asked Wink. He tried to picture Sticky making brogues and boots.

"Lumbnut was his name. When he'd been too long at the *poteen*, I called him Dumbnut behind his back."

Mungo chuckled. He was certain Sticky was lying. Sure, and wouldn't a long wild tale postpone his trip? Still, he could forgive her anything when she made him laugh.

"Old Dumbnut and I lived in a gully, where we made shoes at night. On squallish days, he hooked a crock of gold dust to his suspenders and went to the end of the rainbow. He buried the fortune and waited for a mortal to find it, though no one ever did. While he was gone, I had to tidy up the ditch. On his return, I polished his boots and washed the dirt off the gold.

"'Twas such a nasty job, always cleaning after someone else! And faery spit wouldn't do for Dumbnut's boots—he made me use black polish. It stained my hands, as did the filthy gold. So I ran away to become a Banshee.

"It was dreadful hard to start over. I had to leave everything behind except my needle. But part of a Banshee's job is washing shrouds, you see. I hoped the constant scouring would clean my hands. Nothing helped—not even the bark scrubber I used."

Sticky took off the gloves and turned her palms face up. Wink stared at the deformity.

"Ewww," he whispered. "Nasty."

Blushing with embarrassment, Sticky promptly sat upon her hands.

Oh dear, oh dear, thought Mungo. *This fantasy has gone too far.* He knew of Banshees. Handmaidens of Death, they announced his presence with a low, mournful call. Most often they were seen on a rock near a dying person's house, washing and wailing. But weren't they winsome lasses? With goldish locks that tipped the ground? Sticky was plain of face, and her hair sprouted like a tussock of grass.

"Sticky," he said carefully, "Banshees are known for their beautiful tresses. Your hair is most attractive, my dear, but . . ."

"My hair was perfection, Mungo, perfection! How I loved to groom it with the silver comb. Still, I grew sick of serving Death — the scrubbing, the constant traveling from house to house. And the wailing nearly wrecked my voice. That's when I went to the smokestack to join the Nuckelavees."

"Nuckelavees!" Wink said. "What *were* you thinking?"

"How can I make you understand? I knew they were cruel as storms. But by then, I was desperate to live someplace other than a ditch or rock. Wanting only to settle down on a ledge of my own, you see."

Tears of frustration rolled down Sticky's cheeks. Mungo gave her a handkerchy.

"Blow," he ordered.

She honked. "At first the Nuckelavees turned me down. The one named Nigel said I wasn't mean enough. When I promised to make fancy shoes for them, they agreed to let me in, and at the next full moon, we gathered for my Reduction. The ceremony required that I strip the gloves.

"But it was all over when the vagabones saw my hands. They roosted on my ears chanting, "'Isn't she the dirty one? Can't get clean!'"

Wink remembered the guttural sound of Nuckelavees in battle. "Your ears — how frightening!"

"Nuckelavees think they're upper class, you see, and won't tolerate differences of any sort. One laughed and called me Sticky. Then Nigel laid on a Reverting Curse. If I were to change the name, everything I touched would revert to me. 'Twould stick like wax. Soon I'd suffocate from the weight."

"Glic, glic," Wink sympathized.

"You know, I'm not one to lose my temper, but I couldn't help myself. Spit on every one o'them, I did."

At this, Mungo burst out laughing.

Sticky glared at him. "Nigel complained to the Dallahan. He said only a low-class faery would stoop to spitting. So that very night, the Chief put me on a falcon and banished me to West Isle for five winters as punishment. I managed to bring the comb and needle, but on the way, I had to disguise my former identity. Turn my Banshee gown into a cloud . . ." — Sticky stumbled over the awful memory — ". . . and ask a hawk to chew off my hair."

Mungo looked out the door. A cold new moon was tilting toward Mully Mountain. "It's late. I must place the sleeping pebble in Eamon's ear."

Wink thought back to Sticky's arrival and counted on his fingers. "Five winters. This means the exile is over."

"On Midsummer's Day." Sticky lowered her eyes and picked at her nails. "The Chief offered me a deal. He said I could be a Banshee emeritus. Have long golden hair again and retire to my own ledge in the smokestack. But only if I bring a human boy back with me. A strong one as tall as a mortal's broom.

Mungo leapt into the air. Suddenly the puzzle fell into place. Sticky's mysterious appearance on West Isle. Her obsession with Eamon. Even her deep voice. "Holy Moses! Your story is true! And it's Eamon, is it? You're taking the lad to that wretched hive of Solitary Ones?"

For the briefest moment, Sticky looked as sad as the wind. "Every so often, the Chief requires a mortal child who is well to look upon, for strengthening the line, you see. Once Eamon is grown, he will be Reduced, then matched with a Nuckelavee woman."

"Eamon a Nuckelavee!" cried Mungo. "It's unthinkable!"

"I agreed to the deal but only if . . . if Eamon could be my exclusive servant forever."

Sticky closed her eyes. Pleasure crept, snakelike, into her voice. "What a lovely revenge. Imagine — my own private Nuckelavee to sweep the ledge, bring the food, wash my acorn. Won't that set the little darlings off, seeing one of their own as a servant? And to crown the thing, I'll finally have a place to call home.

"The smokestack won't be ideal, but what is? I'll brighten the ledge with pillows, weave a rug perhaps. And I'll always have Eamon to keep me company, though he won't look like himself, of course."

The faery struggled to find her feelings. "Only lately it seems . . . Eamon's a good lad, he is. Listen, Mungo, you must protect him. When the Nuckelavees attack, they won't know he is my chosen one. The thought of their swords stabbing his neck . . ."

Mungo's earlobes trembled. "Or the thought of losing a servant!"

Wink stared at Sticky. "Aye, it's for her own good that the cat purrs. Sticky, you've been a Trooping Faery for five years. Worn our clothes, walked our secret paths, used our magic. If you steal the boy for wicked reasons, it puts disgrace and a bad name on all of us. And maybe you *are* a spy! How do we know you haven't brought the famine?"

"I knew nothing of it!" protested Sticky. "Mungo, surely you don't think . . . ?"

Mungo strapped on his pouch. "No, but you *have* lied to us about your past. And now I bid you goodbye, Sticky the Shoemaker, Banshee, Nuckelavee, whatever you are. Wink, take her to the Queen's castle."

"Wait!" Sticky cried. She lifted the quartz looking glass from the wall and dropped it in Mungo's pouch. "If a Nuckelavee corners you, shine this in its face. You will be saved, I swear it."

With a dark look at the friend who had betrayed him, Mungo buttoned his cloak and adjusted his cap. And in the time it takes for a raindrop to fall, he was gone.

May Day

To this blessed day, I have trouble telling of the May Day battle, and I being a *seanchaí*! All I can say is that by nightfall the wind was screeching like ten thousand crows. 'Twas so loud that a brace of *pookas*, out to enjoy the waxing of the moon, gathered in the trench of a cloud and watched the drama unfold.

At long and at last, a phalanx of Nuckelavees flew into the air space over Frog Leg Island. The Trooping Ones were prepared. Eamon had reknotted the nets, and in case of capture, the faeries had stuffed their pouches with a month's supply of dried herring. The Queen was prepared—the Weapon of Last Resort hung by her side in a deerskin scabbard. Eamon was ready, too, for Mungo had trained him well.

"I hear them!" bellowed the Queen. "Hie over cap!" At this signal, Eamon yanked a clump of fern from the earth and mounted it. "Borram! Borram! Borram!"

Holding the reins in one hand, he waved a hurling stick above his head with the other. It was the bravest sight alive—that treasure of a boy, leading an army of faery men and women up into the air, and the Queen riding alongside.

"Watch out!" Jam warned when the Nuckelavees came close. "They've pikes on their shoulders!"

"Yerra!" cried a Thrower. "Do ye see the shields of ice

on their arms? Our darts will bounce off like hurling balls!"

"Keep the nets high," Mungo urged. "Move in only when I raise my hand. . . . Now!"

The Trooping Faeries caught thousands of the savages, and Eamon swatted hundreds with his stick, yet countless more surged out of the darkness. A good number of Wee Ones were injured by the flying pikes. Many fell back to Frog Leg, where to this day they outrun the rats and wait for orders from the Queen.

One of the *pooka* men shook his head at the carnage below. "Doesn't look good for the Trooping Ones."

"'Tis a shame," harrumphed another. "Haven't they always shown us the greatest respect?"

"We've missed one ball already," said a *pooka* woman. "If they lose, who will dance with us next Hallow Eve?"

That settled it. The *pookas* turned themselves into a herd of black ponies with shaggy manes and red eyes. Down through the clouds they went, soaring headlong into the confusion. "Hop on!" the *pooka* ponies called to a cluster of Nuckelavees. "You can ride us into the heart of the battle!"

The tiny knaves climbed aboard, but ho! Didn't the ponies promptly turn around and bolt from the fight! Eyes burning and tongues aflame, they carried the Nuckelavees to East Isle and dumped them in a sewer.

Back in the skies over Frog Leg, still more of the beasties riz up all in a line. Desperate, the Queen drew forth her weapon. On seeing this, Jam went against the very grain of his obedient nature. "No, my Queen! It might be the end of you!"

"Jam, take my reins," she calmly ordered. "Trooping Ones! Hold fast to one another!"

The Queen filled her lungs with air, lifted a heavy bronze horn to her lips, and blew. Blanching with the effort, she blew once more, until her chest caved in and all the blood vessels in her eyes broke.

Mercy upon us all, you never want to hear such a sound. Many miles away in Knockabeg, mortals fell to their knees, certain the hour of their death was at hand. Several roofs collapsed, and even the springhouse walls crumbled to the ground.

Meanwhile the vibration shook the Nuckelavees' bodies as if they were fiddle strings. It set off a burning in their bowels, right enough. Crazed from the pain, they flew into one another like a swarm of bees.

That's when Mungo saw him. Leading one last band of Nuckelavees was Nigel from the smokestack. A stiff new wing sprouted from his side. And didn't he get tearing mad when he spied the Queen's battle horn!

"That one!" Nigel cried. His troops lifted their pikes and pointed them directly at the Queen's head.

There was no time for wisdom, or Mungo might have considered the danger. "Jam! Cover me!"

While Jam's shooters pelted the Nuckelavees with darts, Mungo up and give a whilloo. He rushed the demon man, and for fastness, you never saw such an assault as that.

With a scream, Nigel landed on the nape of Mungo's neck and began to chew his flesh. "This one, too!"

Mungo shook his head violently from side to side, but

he couldn't dislodge the shrew's sharp tiny teeth. "Tarnation seize ye!" he thundered.

Suddenly Mungo remembered Sticky's looking glass. He pulled it from his pouch and angled it over his shoulder. When Nigel saw his own face, glory be, if he didn't stop to smile at himself! The Nuckelavee was still spellbound as a net caught him like a crab, and he clawing to break free.

Frantically Mungo galloped through the remaining Nuckelavees. He shone the mirror in each of their faces, until the nets held every grinning one o'them.

"Heave ho!" Jam cried. The Trooping Ones slung the nets toward the far side of the moon, then fell forward with relief upon their horses' necks. Though it's meself that says it, I do think they deserved to close their eyes and float among the clouds for a trifle of rest.

The deep indigo skies then turned strangely silent, as if the clouds were waiting for something to happen. Eamon wiped wing specks from his stick and trotted over to his teacher.

His blue eyes were sparkling, for didn't riding a horse in the sky remind him of fishing from the high cliffs? Aye, he could remember everything grand about his mortal life, yet nothing of Da and Granny's deaths or the gloomy cabin he'd left behind.

"How did I do, Mr. Mungo?"

Before Mungo could answer, Jam's voice ripped through the air. "The Queen has collapsed!"

With great speed, Eamon galloped to her side and caught her hand as she slid from the horse. "Easy now,"

Jam cautioned. Carefully removing her glasses, he hoisted her into Eamon's arms.

"Aye, sir." The boy held the Queen lightly, for in regard to size, she reminded him of Hannah as a babe.

"What now, Mungo?" panted Jam.

"Fly down to base camp?"

Jam's mind was in a ponder. Without orders, he scarcely knew what to do. "Perhaps that's best. I need to pick up Frankie, anyway. But what do ye think Herself would want?"

"If you please, sir," offered Eamon, "maybe she should come home with me. When I'm ailing, a mouthful of tea sets me right. My Granny would wipe the creepy for your Queen. Give her a dry seat by the fire and a sup and sip of everything she needs."

"You're nicer than that puppy Frankie Blaine," remarked Jam. "Too bad. I wish you could be ours forever."

Mungo thought of Sticky's plan to possess the boy. "Eamon doesn't belong to anyone, except his mother and sister."

"And Da and Granny," Eamon added.

"Ah," said Mungo sadly. "If only I could make it so." He took the Queen from Eamon and placed the sleeping pebble in his ear.

Perhaps we should *return to Knockabeg*, the faery thought. *The laddie has earned a reward, and all too soon he'll have to reenter the mortal world.* And soon Mungo would have to turn Sticky in as a spy.

Who will decide her fate? he wondered. *The Queen is in no shape to lead us now.*

These thoughts troubling him, Mungo tucked the Queen under one arm and Eamon under the other. "Rouse yourselves, my friends," he called to the Trooping Faeries. "We're going home."

Yawning and stretching, the Wee Ones nudged their horses and began the long trip back. They reached Knockabeg at dawn, just as a waterfall of sunlight poured over the valley. Tired past all imagining, they slipped into their caves, shrugged off their pouches, and closed the doors tight.

Ye may be wondering about the fate of Frankie Blaine. Wait now, and I'll tell ye. As Mungo and the troops were heading home, Jam flew down to Frog Leg. By now, Frankie was stiff as a peg leg, having been tied up during the battle, you see.

"Mother," Frankie sobbed on seeing Jam. "I want me mother!" he sobbed.

"O ho! Don't we all?" Jam unknotted the vines that held Frankie to the gravestone. "You're going home, my beauty, but here's the situation. When we leave, you can't look back. Else you'll remember your time with the faeries, and we can't have that."

Jam put Frankie under his arm and plucked a yellow ragweed.

"Do you promise not to look?" asked the faery.

"I never will at all."

"Yellow ragweed, be a horse under me!"

Isn't curiosity the most curious thing? As the horse rose into the air, Frankie did look down at Frog Leg Island. Two seconds later, he'd grown a broccoli for a brain and a brussels sprout for a nose.

"That'll teach you to meddle and moil with a faery," said Jam, but the stunned Frankie didn't hear a word of it. By blare of day, he was back in his cabin, where the Blaines found him sitting lopsided in a meal barrel, a broccoli leaf growing from his ear. And that was that.

As the Blaines stared at their eejit son, Eamon was waking up. And where should he be but inside a great hall, stretched out on a bed of feathers? Comfortable as a prince, he was, and the same size as the faeries.

Eamon opened his eyes and looked around. A vaulted ceiling soared above his head, its vast space lit by hundreds of lanterns hanging from the walls. Against one wall stood two pillars that marked a passage to the outside world. Against the other wall was a table piled high with dried herring, the usual feast being impossible, of course.

Faery couples were reeling all about to the sound of fiddles, drums, whistles, and fifes. "Hup! Ho!" they cried, excited to be home after six months of war.

"By the powers, where am I?" cried Eamon.

Mungo was crouched next to the boy's bed. "You're in the Queen's castle, lad. You'll rest here until dusk, then I'll take you home."

"How is Her Honor?"

Mungo hesitated. He didn't want to ruin his gift to the lad. "She's conscious now, but don't worry yourself. Just be enjoying the music." Mungo pointed to the balcony where the faery band perched. Eamon's eyes followed.

Well, ye won't believe it, and Eamon didn't either. Next

to the whistle player stood a fellow in a fisherman's knitted sweater. With him was a white-haired lady, plump as an apple. To Mungo's surprise, a dark-haired beauty suddenly appeared between them. A soft wool shawl was draped around her shoulders.

Eamon jumped up, every eye in his head as big as the bowl of a spoon. "Da? Granny? Mamaí?"

"How are all the bones in your body, me boy?" Da called.

"It's a grand time, you're having, is it?" asked Mamaí.

"Come down and I'll tell you about the battle!" Eamon said. "Oh, I was the brave one, I was!"

Before you could crack two turkey eggs, the family had hopped to the floor. While Granny laid a smack of a kiss on Eamon's cheek, Da gave him a meaty hug, and Mamaí tickled him until he wriggled away, laughing. Jerusalem, such a sight they were, the mother, father, granny, and son. It makes my eyes go moist just to remember it.

The foursome settled happily on giant toadstools under the balcony. As Eamon told how he had swung a hurling stick with all the veins of his heart, the grownups' faces brightened with pride. When he was finished, a waiter served herring, and they all set to.

Alas, hours pass like minutes in a faery castle. The visit was soon over. Mungo buttoned his cape and toddled over to the mortals. "It's time, Eamon."

Eamon stepped aside to let Granny go first. He took Da's right hand and Mamaí's left. "Lead the way, Mr. Mungo. We'll follow."

Mamaí stroked her boy's face. "Eamon, as the old cock crows, the young cock learns. Listen for a moment to your Da and Granny."

"Son," said Da, "you'll be man-big soon. When the time comes, remember this: you'll never plow a field by turning it over in your mind."

Granny ruffled her grandson's hair. "Eamon, my treasure, it's you who will be the long-headed one in the cabin. Mind Da's advice and this, too: it's no use boiling your cabbage twice."

"Will ye not be coming with me?"

Mamaí gave him a tender kiss. "Sure, we might be seeing you later."

As Mungo led Eamon away, the lad turned to wave goodbye. The last he saw of his kin, they were dancing a wild jig. And the last faery he saw was sitting by the exit.

Wink stood next to her with a bunch of nettle leaves on the end of a pitchfork. There was no need to bind a prisoner under house arrest. The sting of the hairy leaves would stop any criminal, you see. Sticky was too weak to go far, anyway—to prove she hadn't brought the famine, she'd refused to eat any herring at all.

When Eamon came nigh, the faery woman leaned toward him. Wink gave the nettles a warning shake. "Let me look at your face!" she called to the boy. "I cannot part with you, oh dream of my heart!"

"Hush, traitor!" Mungo ordered. Quickly he placed the faery pebble in Eamon's ear. In three hops of a sparrow the laddie-buck was dozing on the floor.

"Mungo," Sticky said, begging, "let me go to the cabin with Eamon. You don't know why Mamaí has joined Granny and Da. Tell him, Wink."

Wink's face turned moss green. "As I was marching Sticky here to the castle, we passed Blaine's field. Mamaí was on all fours, gnawing . . ." Wink stopped, too sick to go on.

". . . gnawing the carcass of a rotten hen," finished Sticky. "The hen had died of Catching Fever. It's running wild through Knockabeg. Mamaí must have caught it and died. If Hannie ate the chicken, too . . ."

"Can nothing be done, Wink?" asked Mungo.

"If Hannah is sick, one of Sticky's herb mixtures might help. But remember — if we let her go and she steals the boy at midsummer, she might put a bad name on all us Trooping Ones."

"Aye," Mungo agreed. The music broke off, and he and Wink looked toward the balcony. There stood Jam, cap in hand.

"Good People," he announced. "The Queen's condition is worse. Go home now, and wish on a star for her. Wink and Mungo, she wants to see the Steps immediately."

Well, ye must have guessed what happened then, but I'll tell ye anyway. When Mungo and Wink looked back, they saw the bottom of Eamon's bare feet disappearing through the passage. Sticky was gone, and she dragging the boy behind her like a sack of oats.

———

Mungo was furious at Sticky, but it passed when he entered the Queen's chamber. This was the first time he'd been invited, and who could stay angry in such a place?

The ceilings were draped with sky-blue silk. Mats woven of thyme softened the stone floor. A star chip glowed from the ceiling, bathing the room in a cool light.

The Queen's bedstead was most royal—constructed of dwarf willow, it was piled high with layers of goose down. Though she lay prostrate upon the bed, and her red-streaked eyes were now thoroughly blind, Mungo thought Herself had never looked more queenly. She motioned to the mats. The Steps sat down, their faces solemn.

The Queen was wheezing. "I need your thoughts before I send for Sticky."

The Steps glanced at one another. Hadn't they all agreed to keep Sticky's treason from the Queen until she was well?

"Your Honor, I know you want to punish her," said Mungo, "but I'm afraid she's escaped."

"I do not wish to punish her! If you agree, I want her to succeed me!" Mungo scratched his head. So the Queen didn't know, after all.

Jam spoke slowly, reluctant to upset his leader. "My Queen," he said, "Mungo said Sticky was a Solitary One. A Leprechaun, then a Banshee, and almost a . . . a Nuckelavee!"

A smudge of color appeared in the Queen's cheeks. "Tell me something new. I suspected as much when she first arrived."

"How did you know?"

"Because I guessed that Solitary Ones must also be lonely ones, and I'd never seen a Trooping One as lonely as she."

"Or as impudent!"

"But who was I to deny our friendly world to someone in need? After she banished the Willy Wisps, I knew she could be trusted."

The Queen's breath was coming hard and fast. "The Nuckelavees may be back. As a Solitary One, Sticky is familiar with their thinking, their magic. Since I can no longer see, she must be my eyes."

"But my Queen, you don't know the whole sorry story," said Mungo. He then revealed Sticky's plan to turn Eamon into a Nuckelavee. To be fair, he also explained her deep affection for Hannah.

The Queen's color was fading. "Ah. If Sticky loves Hannah, she may do the right thing yet, but watch her carefully. Wait until Midsummer's Eve. If she tries to steal the boy, intervene."

"And if she leaves him here?" asked Jam.

"Then her sacrifice deserves our highest regard, and you must beg her to take my place."

Mungo hung his head. Sure, and Herself held such wisdom that there was no coming up to it.

Wink puffed up like a dandelion in flower. So proud he was of the insult he'd thrown at Sticky in the springhouse that he repeated it now. "Sticky will steal him, I'm sure. She'll never get back to Above-the-Sky."

The Queen's eyelids fluttered. "Wink, your words may be wiser than you know. The Trooping Ones have been unselfish in this war, but perhaps it isn't enough. Perhaps Sticky was sent to us for a reason, though who can be sure of these things? She is not a Trooping Faery, but she has lived as one for five winters. If she gives up the boy, she might fully redeem us. Then we can *all* reenter Above-the-Sky . . ."

With these words, the faery leader's weakened lungs gave out. Her head rolled sideways on the pillow, and she fell into a white, blank sleep that seemed to be the cousin of Death, if not the man himself.

Well, so, and on to Sticky. Her escape had put her in a pretty pickle, for when she exited the castle door, she was too feeble to hop. Dizzy from the hunger strike, she cast herself upon the steep bank that formed the front wall of the castle.

Eamon lay full-sized in a pile at her feet. "Whatever will I do with you?" she asked, as if the boy could hear her. "I'm near two days fasting and cannot carry you."

Out of habit, her fingers moved to trace the *S* on her cape. "Oh, dear me." It hurt to remember how Wink had torn off her initial. But touching the lapel gave her an idea, and within five flicks of a puppy's ear the cape was a stretcher. "Come on, love," she said to Eamon, "'tis only three miles, and I know a shortcut across a faery pass. We'll make it yet."

The lad turned out to be a heavier load than ever Sticky

thought, but by and by she crossed the bridge near his house. Now, suppose the moon had not been playing Barney-Barney-Buck-and-Doe with the clouds that night. Suppose the sky had not gone black dark just as Sticky passed Blaine's wall. She might have seen the horseshoes stuck between the loose stones, and me story might have a different ending entirely.

Instead, she came within inches of the wicked iron. Pain instantly blasted her temples, and she fell to her knees. "Blaine, you dirty rip!"

And suppose the oldest Carr boy hadn't been guarding his field with a musket, though I should say more sleeping than guarding was going forward. When Sticky's cry made his nose itch, he awoke and looked down the hill.

"Why, 'tis a rabbit, after our petatie vines!" yelled the sharp-eyed fellow. 'Twas only a boy asleep on a faery cape, but the young man fired, indeed he did. "Ha! I done you, rabbit, clever as you think you are!"

The musket ball just missed Eamon's ear and left a scorch on Sticky's cheek. She touched the burn with horror. "Haven't I trouble enough?" she shrieked at the Carr boy. "By the devil, you'll pay for this!"

With a last sliver of strength, Sticky half-crawled into Eamon's yard, the stretcher clutched in one hand. Blue ribbons of dawn streaked the sky, and somewhere off toward Kiltymore a cock crowed. Knockabeg was waking up, but when she reached the cabin, there was no stir of life about the place. The faery woman shoved the door open and peered inside.

Hannah lay on the floor, fast asleep. The child's cheeks were hollow, and her nose had a pinched look. One wee fist clutched the leg of the spinning wheel. The other was stuck in her mouth.

"*Ach*, little one," whispered Sticky. "You've the face of an old woman, but at least you're alive."

Shaky with hunger, Sticky rolled Eamon off the cape. She then curled up inside the dresser, where she had fretful dreams about a boy, a whip, and eyes the color of pus.

"In the name o'goodness, Eamon, get up." A tall, stoop-shouldered priest stood in the cabin door. "Where've ye been these three days?"

Father Gallagher leaned over and shook Eamon's shoulder. "Do ye think I cannot smell the herring on your breath? Stealing food for yourself, you were, while your *mamaí* . . ."

The lad blinked himself awake. Confused, he glanced around. "What of Mamaí?"

Gallagher sat down heavily on the edge of the outshot. Hunger pangs were cutting deep into his belly. "Sure, it must be the will o'God, the way people are dropping off. Yesterday I came by here with a noggin of meal and a few pieces of turf. Your dear mother was in fever. She was called from this life while I heard her confession."

Eamon's head jerked, as if the side of a spade had whacked him. How could the boy understand such great tragedy, when the priest himself didn't know, except to say it was the will of God?

"Son, fever victims must be buried straight away. I sent for a cart. Your *mamaí* is at rest at the bottom of the field, by the boulder."

"Did Hannah see . . . ?"

"She slept through it all. I begged Margaret Carr to take her, but the woman was most afraid of catching the sickness.

"I had others to tend to, and no choice but to leave Hannah sleeping here. Aye, it's bad times, all out. Now you've a decision to make, Eamon. The people are reduced to eating chickweed — stay, and you and Hannah will likely starve. Thousands are fleeing West Isle every day. Like them, you could take a ship across the ocean to Great Land. But you lack the fare and are too young to go alone."

The priest put his hands together and uttered a silent prayer. Mother o'God, it was hard to say the next words.

"Or you could go to the workhouse in Kiltymore. For cutting turf, they'll give you bread and sugar water. You must go soon if you want a space. The building is a sprawling thing, but already it's overcrowded."

Gallagher couldn't bring himself to tell Eamon the worst of it. That people were shaking the gates to get in the workhouse, though there the living lay for days on the same straw as the dead. That corpses, may the saints protect them, were tossed down a chute from the second floor, and a cart driver dumped them in a pit at the edge of town. The people knew it was a place of death. Yet ofttimes hunger is stronger than anything, even reason.

Eamon scratched his itching foot and looked hopelessly

at the priest. "Sure, and I don't know what to say. How can I leave me mother a'laying in the ground, all alone? And Da built this cottage with his own hands. Don't Shank's men pull down the walls after a tenant . . . ?"

Hannah awoke then with a cry, she with the starvation pressing most keenly upon her. The priest hurried to boil the meal he'd brought the day before, and Eamon went outside.

He kicked the bench by the door, for what else can a troubled boy do? From his heart out, he wept for his *mamaí*, for Hannah who was screaming inside, for himself who could not make up his mind.

Now what happened as the lad cried is still a mystery. But soon and after a while, the tempest of tears spent itself. Though his head felt most split from the hard grieving, he went in and stood tall before the priest.

"I'll never plough a field by turning it over in my mind. I've made up me mind. We'll not give up the land or the cabin. If we die, we die here in Da's house."

Well, in my experience, life can turn as quickly as a mountain path, and sometimes it happens that good follows bad.

The Lord and Lady Shank had grown most sick of the sight of little skeletons wandering the parish roads. And so it was that the next day, when Father Gallagher found the children weeping by their mother's grave, he could give them glad news: any child attending the local school would receive free food from Shank.

The priest sent the children off to school with a blessing,

then went up to see about the shouts from the Carr cabin. Some claim revenge is sweet, but you'll have to ask a certain faery about that. I'm only the *seanchaí*, and I couldn't say.

When the priest reached the yard, he found the family standing outside in a sorry state. The eldest son was pouring brown filth from his shoe like it was tea from a pot. Margaret was wringing liquid from the hem of her dress. "Ah, Father, I woke this morning to find me cabin floor covered in a pool of dung!"

"We're after leaving this cursed place," said her second boy.

"When the spuds are big enough to dig," vowed the youngest, "it's to Great Land we're going!" Margaret, who hated to see a feather stuck to an egg, much less dung on her clean floor, nodded in agreement.

The Carrs were not the only ones to suffer Sticky's wrath. When Eamon and Hannah arrived at school in a driving rain, the teacher tried to block the door.

I suppose it'd do my soul good to forgive Samuel Love — after all, the room was built for only one hundred, and now 'twas packed with almost two hundred gaunt children. The air was stifling, and Love's collar was clammy with the sweat.

"You've not come since your da . . . well, in over a year," Love complained to Eamon. "If the likes of you fill up the school, where will we put respectable children?"

Then didn't Love feel a hot breath on his right cheek? And didn't a nice fat tumor, round as a penny, appear upon the spot? Everyone in Knockabeg understood that only a faery can put a blast on your face. Knowing he was faery-struck, and terrified of losing his good looks entirely, the teacher pushed two pupils off a bench and invited Eamon and Hannah to sit.

That was the end of it. Every Friday when school let out, the children received two noggins of broth and six pounds of biscuits each. By the first of June, Hannah's cheeks were rounder, and she looked like a little girl again. When her feet started to grow she took off her boots, though she wouldn't let Eamon give them away.

Eamon throve too. He even felt well enough to cut turf. One evening Sticky followed close behind as he headed home from the bog. Gloating, she observed his calves, his arms, the easy way he carried the weight of the cutting tool on his shoulder. "By the cross, I've done it! Hannah is strong enough to take care of herself, and Eamon is growing again. By Midsummer's Eve, he'll be ready for me to steal!"

And so he was.

Midsummer's Eve, Dusk

The truth is in my mouth when I say this Midsummer's Eve was as soft as those in the rare old times. The sky ached with blue; the pastures were green and fine. But I will not lie to ye about the rest.

No one was strong enough to welcome new crops with the usual bonfire. At day-most-gone, no dancers leapt around the flames, bodies supple as rushes, faces aglow. The truth is, there were few crops growing at all.

Now, 'tis true that potato vines reached proudly toward the June sun in the Carrs' field. The boys had already dug and sacked baby tatties for the voyage the next day. Margaret was dreadful sorry to leave the land of her birth, but her sons were lighthearted with the adventure they saw before them.

Sticky was feeling light as a waltz, too. According to her estimate the night before, Eamon had grown the length of two June bugs. He was now taller than a broom. "This time tomorrow," she crowed from inside the dresser, "I'll be combing my hair on a private ledge. And soon after, I'll have a servant of me own. Me! Sticky! The faery they called the Dirty One!"

As dusk arrived, Sticky waited for Eamon to return from the bog. Licking her lips, she checked her pouch. "Let me see. A sleeping pebble. Five biscuits saved from the windowsill. Ten darts, just in case." Though Sticky didn't expect trouble. Indeed, she'd seen no Wee Ones at all since her escape.

Ah, but they were watching for *her*. "Wink," Mungo called from a space inside the ruined springhouse, "there's a good stand of ragweed growing here. How goes it with you?"

Wink answered from the putrid potato pit. Two rosebuds were stuffed in his nostrils. "The ferns are thick and deep, but she'll not get her hands on them."

"Ho, Jam!" Mungo called to the dung heap. "Can ye stand the stink?" Jam, who was deep inside the pile of mortal waste, couldn't answer. An oak leaf was strapped over his nose and mouth, you understand. Still, he'd make sure no rush of straw from the thatched roof carried Eamon to East Isle that night.

So, while evening folded around the mountain peaks, the Steps waited for a faery woman needing a horse, and Sticky waited for Eamon. During these quiet moments, the faery let herself think of Hannah. "She'll be a mite lonely at first," Sticky worried aloud. "I suppose I could leave her outside the Queen's castle door. The Wee Ones will let her in for a while."

Suddenly a melody began to play deep within the faery woman's brain. She bounced on one foot and stood on her head, but still the notes rattled like rosary beads in a box. "What on earth? Is it Jimmy's 'Lord Shank'?"

Sticky slapped her face to rid herself of the lament. She

thought some more. No, the castle would never do. The child could just stay a day or so — only brides or mortals who have met untimely deaths could live with Trooping Ones forever.

"Oh, I guess I could take her with me. But what if the Chief assigns her to work for one of the Mermen, them with their ugly faces?" Minor chords crashed in Sticky's head. No, she remembered those goons from the smokestack. She couldn't picture Hannah with one of them.

"I have it!" Sticky cried. "The priest! Gallagher will take care of her, surely."

Never mind that the man had all of Knockabeg to worry about, and little time for another orphan child. Sticky knew this full well. Isn't it peculiar, the lies we can tell ourselves?

Finally, impatient with the music that pounded her head, Sticky hopped out of the dresser. "I can't wait any longer, me boy. I'm coming after you. Get ready for a snooze!"

But Sticky hadn't counted on passing by Hannah's boots. The charming things were sitting on the flag of the hearth. Inside one was a bunch of eye-bright flowers. "Faith," Sticky said, moaning.

She turned the boots over in her hands and proceeded to slip one in her pouch. "I'll just take it to remember her by."

Then such a start she never got as when Hannah appeared, crying, at her side. "No! No! You gave me them boots. Can't have them back!"

Glic! Had Granny passed the Sight on to Hannie? Desperate to stop her tears, Sticky set the wee boot down.

Hannah hiccoughed. "Have you seen me *mamai*? I be looking for her everywhere."

Sticky stared up at the child. Aroo, it seemed strange to converse with a mortal. What's more, the faery had no time for it. "Indeed, I saw your mother last month. Living in a castle, she is, just like the gentry."

Hannah held out a grubby, half-eaten biscuit. "Eamon says she went away because she was sick from the hunger. If you give her this, maybe she can come home."

What good would it do to tell the girl such a thing was impossible? Sticky tapped her foot and looked with longing at the door. "Perhaps. Now run along to the church and find Father Gallagher. I have to go."

"Where's yourself slipping out to?"

Sticky strapped on her pouch. "Oh, um, I have to see about a horse." Werra! Was there any way in the world to stop the girl's questions?

"You have pretty hands."

"They're *not* pretty. No one else thinks so."

"They *are*! I seen them take food from the windowsill. And last night, they patted Eamon on the head while he was asleep. I wish *I* had golden hands."

"Dirty hands."

Hannah stamped her foot. "Pretty hands!"

The sweetness of the child's compliment made Sticky's head swim. At the same time, she felt a lonely note loosen in her head. It flew out her ear, rolled across the floor, and landed in a corner, where it throbbed like a heartbeat. Then painfully, like the turn of a key in a rusty lock, the weight of exile came unstuck, too.

Hannah slipped her fingers between Sticky's grimy ones. 'Twas a dainty touch, as soft as lamb's wool. Several quiet minutes passed while the girl stroked and played with the faery's hands. Neither said even a small piece of a word.

It was a long way that Sticky went in her mind, but at last she came back to herself with a long sigh. Hannah leaned down and rubbed the faery's head, as if she understood her dilemma. "After you brought the boots, Granny made faery butter from mushrooms. She dabbed it on my eyes. So I could see you, she said, since you be part of the family."

"But I'm not."

"Are too!"

No, Eamon is your real family, thought Sticky. Riven with doubt, she considered her life on East Isle. What if the pleasure of revenge was as brief as the mortals' summer? She'd seen how the leaving of those gentle months always left humans crabby and wanting more. *Just like the Nuckelavees,* she thought, *with their appetite for destruction.* Was it worth sacrificing Hannah and Eamon to find out?

Now. I'm just a tired old *seanchai,* but I do know this: The longest road out is the shortest road home. Through five hard years of exile, Sticky had clung to her desires. Only when she let them go for a moment could she see how hollow they were. And in that instant the way became clear.

"Eamon said he'd look for fir wood in the bog today,"

Hannah said. "To make a stool just for me, so I can sit at Mamaí's spinning wheel. I love Eamon. Do you?"

"I think . . . well, *love* is a strange word, isn't it? I know little of it."

Gently, so as not to leave a mark, Sticky hugged Hannah and kissed her fingers. "I care about both of you, my sweet."

Taking one last look around the dim cabin, the faery let go of Hannah and hopped through the door. "Farewell, Hannie!" she called. "The blessings of the world upon you!" With never a glance over her shoulder, for everyone knows 'tis bad luck to start a journey by looking back, Sticky hopped away.

I still wonder if she knew that Hannah ran after her. Aye, the child's legs pumped until they were too tired to take another step. Or if Eamon knew why he suddenly had to rub his nose there in the bog, as Sticky waved both arms and called goodbye.

But I don't wonder that Sticky decided to go back to East Isle by herself and become a master Leprechaun. After all, she was a fugitive. She could stay in Knockabeg only so long before Wink and his pitchfork of nettles claimed her.

Leaving the wide dark bog behind, Sticky tramped to the open road in search of a fern. *Well and so,* she thought. *I'll spend a few days with Dumbnut to learn the new styles. I'll set up shop in my own ditch . . . bah!* The faery stopped and feverishly scraped the comb through her hair. *Living in a ditch again! I cannot do it.*

She spun back toward the bog. Then didn't she see three wee men appear in the mist ahead of her, each with something in his hand? "By this and that and every other thing," she cried, "the Steps are after me!"

The faery turned and hopped in the other direction. "Bedad and begad! Yon comes Father Gallagher with Margaret Carr, strolling this way. And me without a dresser to hide in."

Sticky was as afraid of the priest as any other faery. Especially when he carried a prayer book, for some Wee Ones swore it gave Gallagher the Sight. With the book in hand, they said, he could spot any Red Cap crossing his path. "He'll cork me in a jar for certain," Sticky groaned.

Turning again, she saw the Steps drawing nigh. "So. Here it is," the faery woman sighed. She sat down in the middle of the road to await her fate. "This is the end."

If the truth must be told, the Steps were just as nervous as Sticky. Only the memory of the Queen lying white and still in the castle gave them the strength to follow her orders.

When they reached Sticky, Jam spoke first. "With all the powers vested in me by the Queen of the Trooping Faeries, I hereby present you with the royal glasses."

Sticky gaped as Jam placed the spectacles on her nose.

Wink went next. "Notwithstanding the foregoing, and in consideration of the afterwards, I do therefore issue to the faery named Sticky a new initial for her cape, embroidered in gold." *To match your hands,* Wink joked to himself. He knew if he said the words aloud that his backside would learn the shape of Mungo's brogue.

Sticky stared in wonderment at the S Wink put in her hand. Mungo was next in line. The Queen's spangly cloak was heavy in his arms. Sticky looked up at him with regret. "Old friend, it's the black shame that's on me for lying to you."

Mungo was not to be outdone by the other Steps in regard to formality. "If it is her will, would the new Queen please rise for the presentation of the cape?"

"What kind of a trick is this?" Sticky asked. "If you want to take me prisoner, play-acting isn't necessary. And if you don't hurry it up, Father Gallagher will take care of us all." She pointed behind her.

Jam peered through the mist. "Wurra!" he cried, hopping in circles. "The man will be on us in ten flips of a trout's tail!"

With one eye on the approaching priest, Mungo hastily explained the Queen's wishes to Sticky. Before she could answer, the priest and Margaret came nigh.

The faeries braced themselves, but the saints be blessed, Gallagher carried no prayer book. Only two paper tickets. "They'll work hard for ye," the priest was arguing. "Hannah is old enough to help cook and clean."

"Me boys won't like it at all. We've barely enough spuds for ourselves," Margaret Carr replied.

"By my vestments, woman! Didn't I beg Lord Shank until he gave me two shiners for the tickets? Had a struggle with Eamon, too. The boy was bent on staying. Said he couldn't leave his mother alone in the field. When I told him there was no use in boiling that cabbage twice, he finally agreed to go."

"They'll not get an extra morsel to eat."

"Just watch over them, won't you? Sure, and they're better off with you in Great Land than here."

"We leave for the Kiltymore dock at dawn. I'm laying it down flat for ye — they must be ready or be left behind."

As the two passed on, Sticky flew into a fit. *Her* children? Going away with *those* boys? Them with their careless gun? All alone in a strange land the tykes would be, without kin or faery or even the priest!

While Sticky ranted up and down the road, Mungo trailed behind. He tried to drape the cape over her shoulders. "You must lead us now," he pleaded.

"We told the *Deenee Shee* to go to the cliff tonight," said Wink. "That they might be meeting their new Queen."

Jam set his jaw. "You must obey, Sticky. This is what Herself wanted."

Defeated, Sticky sat back down in the road. At long and at last she spoke. "Steps," said she, "go to the tower now. Take the glasses and cape with you. Tell the Good People I need time to think. I will be there in five hundred swoops of a hawk."

The Steps did as they were told, but it must be said that all three looked bewildered. Even without the twinkly cape, Sticky already sounded like a Queen.

Midsummer's Eve, Midnight

What I am thinking about now is how the Wee Ones had changed greatly since Hallow Eve. Once again, they put on red caps and headed to the tower. But there was no skipping this time. Thin as thread, they walked single file down the secret paths, most anxious to know if they had a new Queen.

'Twas in everyone's mouth that she might be different somehow. A few had heard she was a Solitary One. Not one of them would let it in their minds there was a scrap of truth to the rumor. But was she kind? Would they have to go to war again?

The flock of faeries reached the field and sat down to worry over these questions. It wasn't a long wait they had before getting the answers. Soon a short figure hopped through the spongy grass.

"Slih, slih," the Wee Ones whispered. "'Tis Sticky."

The Steps came forward to stack themselves, but Sticky waved them away. Silhouetted against the blue-black sky, she climbed the stones alone.

"God save the Queen," Mungo's lone voice called.

"Shray, shray," the Wee Ones answered. How on living earth could Sticky be a queen to them? Everyone knew she was a deserter!

Sticky's voice was so deep that the Wee Ones had to cup

107

their ears. "Good People! I am honored that the Queen trusts me enough to take her place."

"Glic, glic!"

"But I cannot accept. I am not—I never was one of you."

Jam, sensing that confusion might overwhelm the crowd, hopped to the top of the cairn. He knew better than to tell them Sticky had been a Solitary One. Still, he meant to see that all went according to the Queen's plan. "Sticky could have stolen a mortal boy for evil purposes, but she chose not to do it. If she isn't a Trooping Faery, she's just like one!"

The throng caught Jam's passion. "A Trooping Faery! A Trooping Faery!"

"'Tis true about the boy," said Sticky. "And I have enjoyed the company of the High Council." She bent her head gracefully toward the Steps. "Until Wink turned sour with the hunger," she couldn't help but add.

Wink jumped to the top of the cairn. "With all due respect," he retorted, "Sticky was a bit of a back-talker herself."

"This is also true," Sticky admitted to the crowd. "But living here has been difficult. As you know, I don't take well to serving a Queen. And I've tried with little success to adjust to your sociable ways. Twosies and threesies are fine. But the jabbering gossip! It sometimes drives me mad."

"Mad!" the faeries agreed. "Mad!"

Mungo joined the others on top of the rocks. "My friends, do you recall the final conflict with the Nuckelavees?" The crowd grew silent.

"'Twas Sticky's looking glass that saved me, the Queen, all of you."

Pandemonium erupted as the faeries remembered the battle. "Saved us! Saved us! God save our Queen! God save our Queen!"

Oh, why must life be full of hard choices? Sticky wondered. *I suppose I'd have to keep sea beans in my ears, but how sweet it would be to lead these gentle folk . . . and to step on Wink when I want to climb the cairn.*

"We must all face the truth," Sticky said. "My solitary nature cannot be changed. A sparrow cannot be a wren."

She looked at Mungo, her eyes watering. "Nor can a rope be made of sea sand. Somehow I have become tied to my mortal family. It's quite ridiculous, for this is not what I want, but I must go with them. They need me."

"We need you too!" the faeries begged.

Sticky brought the Steps' arms together and raised them. "Help is nearer than you think. Here are your new leaders. A trio of Kings who will act as one, with thrice the wisdom, loyalty . . ."

Sticky made a face. What on earth could she say about Wink? ". . . and personality!"

The Queen who would not be a Queen saluted each Step, then hopped from the cairn. As she passed among the Hill Folk, she waved at each one. "Clah, clah," they cried. "Goodbye! Goodbye!"

Sticky wouldn't let herself turn around. But as she left the field, she heard the Kings struggle to answer a thousand questions at once. *Mungo and Jam will certainly serve the*

Wee Ones well, she decided. And Wink? *Well,* she thought, *faeries do grow up eventually.*

Swiftly, Sticky hopped to Eamon's cabin. Head low, she didn't see the army of six-inch creatures flying over the valley or the potato vines that fainted in their wake. Instead, her heart was full of questions. *Is life only about starting over?* she wondered. *Never easy endings, just hard beginnings?*

Silent as smoke, Sticky slipped into the cabin, where she found Eamon and Hannah asleep by the hearth. Throughout that last night in Knockabeg, the faery kept vigil. Occasionally she brought in a brick of turf and laid it on the fire. There was little else to do for the children—they had nothing at all to pack. Only Hannie's boots, which Sticky knew she would not give up.

Feeling the pangs of an empty belly, the faery opened her pouch and counted her biscuits. "I'll eat just one," she promised herself.

After the past months, Sticky well knew starvation might find her before the journey ended. Aye, she was most a'feared of it. She also knew she could be in the castle at that very moment, wearing a sparkly cloak and bossing Wink. Or sitting on a smokestack ledge, combing her billowing hair.

But if the truth must be told, love is dreadful strong. Especially when it comes slowly, as it did to Sticky. Aye, ofttimes love is more powerful than fear or lost dreams or anything else in the world. Even hunger.

Midsummer's Day

Well and so. The next morning, Father Gallagher arrived at the drizzle of dawn. He walked the children up to the Carr cabin, where they joined Margaret and the boys. The emigrants knelt to receive the priest's blessing, and only Hannah knowing that a faery stood by his foot!

No one else came to bid the group goodbye. Alas, the few mortals who had planted seed potatoes awoke that day to find wilted vines. The poor people stood over their plants with a great weeping and wringing of hands. May the heavens be their bed, none cared if they ever saw Eamon or Hannah or the Carr family again. There was no strength left for caring, you understand.

William Blaine was too tired to notice anything at all, at all. Worn out he was, from the daily pruning of broccoli leaves from his son's ears. And Sheilah, her red hair now worry-gray, had been baking since three in the morn. The missus made a dozen loaves of bread every day, you see. "Faery insurance," she muttered, as she scattered them about the yard.

So the group set off for Kiltymore with little ceremony. Halfway there, the Carr boys decided amongst themselves to take giant steps. Aye, the hooligans meant to leave the children lagging behind.

But didn't Eamon catch up in a hurry, complaining bitterly of itching feet? And didn't Hannah suddenly start to skip? Before long, she was hopping three feet at a time, her left hand gripping the air.

As far as I know, Sticky and the children sailed safely to Great Land. With her by their side, I'm sure they prospered. Until I hear otherwise, I can only hope this was the way it was.

It's for certain that hunger continued in Knockabeg. Many still talk of it, and of the Trooping Ones. How they drifted away because so many mortals died or left. Others say Father Gallagher corked the faeries in jugs, one by one, then buried them under the earth.

Maybe a few made it back to Above-the-Sky, by reason o' Sticky doing the right thing, you see. I can't tell ye for certain what happened to the faeries, but if I were you, I'd heed the oldest mortals of Knockabeg. The ones who survived the famine. They swear if ye see an eddy of dust on the road at night, 'tis a gang of Wee Ones up to a trick.

And mind you, some of the youngest children swear they've spotted Red Caps around Knockabeg. Seen them darting between blackthorn hedges at the foot of Mully Mountain. Indeed, I'm after keeping a crust of bread in my pocket, just in case.

The End

Glossary

A list of Gaelic pronunciations, English definitions, common faery terms, and secret faery words revealed to the author, with a brief review of the laws of Trooping Faery physics.

Ach (AHK): Gaelic word meaning "ah" or "ugh"

Aroo: faery exclamation. Also horo, wurra, werra, whilloo, yerra

Begonies: faery curseword. Also begob, begad, bedad

Bla'guard (BLAG urd): scoundrel

Blatherskite: nonsense

Borram: faery word that turns a fern into a horse

Brogue: stout shoe with hob-nailed sole

Byre: stable for cows, often attached to a cabin

Cairn: large pile of stones

Clah: faery word meaning "goodbye"

Cotter: farmer who rents his land and cottage from a landlord

Creepy: homemade three-legged stool

Deenee Shee (dee nee SHEE): English pronunciation of Gaelic words for "Little People." This species of good faeries are also known as Trooping Ones, Wee Ones, and Good People. Average height is twenty inches.

Dresser: in Ireland, a tall kitchen cabinet. The top shelves are open. Doors enclose the bottom shelves.

Eamon (AY-mun): Gaelic name for "Edward"

Emeritus: retired with honor

Eejit (EE-jit): in Ireland, a person who has done something foolish

Flitch: the side meat of a hog after shoulder, loin, ham, and bones are removed

Gannet: fish-eating seabird

Glic, glic: faery clucking sounds that mean "tsk, tsk"

Gorse: prickly bush with yellow flowers

Hallow Eve: Halloween, or All Saints' Day. The eve of the first day of winter under the old Gaelic calendar.

Hie over cap: faery battle cry

Hurling: Gaelic game similar to field hockey, played with a three-foot stick and nine-inch ball

Hwee: sound of faery laughter

Knockabeg: Gaelic for "little hill"

Mamaí (MAW mee): Gaelic word for "mother"

May Day: May 1. Under the old Gaelic calendar, this was the first day of summer.

Midsummer's Day: middle of the growing season in Ireland. Celebrated on June 24.

Noggin: quart container made of wood

Nuckelavee (NUCK a lah vee): faery belonging to the species known as Solitary Ones (see below). Average length six inches. Called beasties, boogies, bogey-beasts by Trooping Ones.

Ochón (uh CAWN): Gaelic word for "alas"

Outshot: in old Irish cabins, a niche built into the wall to the left of the hearth, reserved for old people who needed the warmth of the fire

Piggin: pint container made of wood

Perch: unit of measurement, about three yards

Pooka (POO kuh): Gaelic word for "ghost"

Poteen (poh CHEEN): Gaelic word for "moonshine," a homemade liquor

Praties: short name for potatoes. Also tatties, petaties, spuds, tubers

Rod: unit of measurement, about five and a half feet

Rood: one fourth of an acre of land

Saint Brigid's Day: February 1. Under the old Gaelic calendar, the first day of spring. Crops were planted around this time.

Saint Stephen's Day: December 26

Skoddy: turnips and oatmeal boiled in water

Sea bean: a seed pod that washes up on shore

Seanchaí (SHAN kee): Gaelic word for "storyteller"

Shray: faery word meaning "no"

Slih, slih: faery words meaning "well, well"

Solitary Ones: faery species that, in the main, is evil. Some, but not all, are winged. Includes Nuckelavees, Sheerie,

Gray Men, Mermen, Willy Wisps, the Dallahan. Height varies. A few in this species, though solitary, are harmless to mortals. These include the Leprechaun and Banshee, whose height averages about one foot.

Teeming the spuds: in Ireland, draining boiled potatoes

Turf: in Ireland, another word for "peat," or compacted plant matter found in wet ground called a "bog"

Weeshy, waushy (WEE shee, WAW shee): faery words meaning "small." Also dony, piggly

Whisht: expression of shock. Literally it means "be quiet."

Willy Wisps: ghostly Solitary Ones whose flickering lights are a sign of restlessness

Laws of Trooping Faery Physics:

- The maximum distance a faery can traverse in one hop is three feet.

- Trooping Faeries cannot fly unless they ride faery horses.

- Faeries are allergic to iron and should avoid it if possible.

- Direct sunlight can be fatal to faeries. They must guard against it at any cost.

- Belled caps provide a veil of invisibility. It is crucial that faeries wear their headgear when mortals are nearby.

- Faeries can eat only food given to them by mortals.

- Faeries cannot fight without a mortal by their side.

- A few rare mortals, usually children, possess the Sight, which allows them to see faeries.

- Only brides and those who have met untimely deaths can live with faeries forever.

- Upon entering a faery castle, mortals automatically return to good health and shrink to faery size.

- Mortal time speeds up within a faery domain. Two minutes pass as two seconds, for example, and two hours pass as quickly as two minutes.

Author's Note

Knockabeg: A Famine Tale was inspired by the worst of the many blights that struck Ireland's potato crops in the nineteenth century. The famine that followed lasted from 1845 to 1852. It left almost 1 million Irish dead from starvation or disease. Another 1.2 million fled the country, followed by 6 million more over the next seventy years. Exiled by hunger, most of these Gaelic-speaking people came to America.

Two of my great-grandmothers and one of my great-grandfathers were infants or children during the famine. For their sakes, I very much wanted to tell a story about what has been called the "Great Hunger."

One golden September day I began the writing of my tale. Yet every time I tried to imagine this awful disaster, my spirits fell. The tears were many; it did not seem possible to write and weep at the same time.

Then a band of faeries appeared outside my window. At first they looked like motes of dust floating in the afternoon sun, until I heard squeals. "Put us in the story, too!" they seemed to say. In need of companionship, and never one to live dangerously, I felt it best to give them their way.